THE RETIREMENT PLAN.

BY JOHN LAMB.

www.jklambauthor.com

INTRODUCTION:

Joan and Brian have been married for almost 40 years and consider themselves to be very ordinary, steady, down to earth, sensible people who have worked all their adult lives, saving money where they could, but always contributing towards their pension so they could be certain of a comfortable and secure old age.

As they approached their retirement age, they began to consider the options of selecting a pension provider but were overwhelmed and confused by the volume of information and quotations presented to them.

The solution appeared when a smart, professional young man arrived at their door and introduced himself as an executive of an international, privately operated investment fund, and presented them with an exciting pension proposal that would not only generate tremendous income returns, but certainty that both the income and capital would be protected with a 'cast iron', inflation proof return, supported by an insurance backed guarantee. It seemed like divine intervention and the answer to their pension needs and much, much more.

As their retirement date approached, they contacted the company to arrange for the pension payments to commence. They heard nothing. After months of futile efforts to locate where their investments had gone, they realised they'd been duped, and nobody could help them. With what little money they had left they recognised it was no longer possible to maintain their current lifestyle for more than a few months.

After much thought they decided their choices were limited to: -

1). Surviving on the meagre State Pension.

2). Continue working.

3). Commit suicide.

4). Create income through other means: -

Legal: -

   a). Put all remaining money either as a bet on a horse or buying lottery tickets.

   b). Start a business.

Illegal: -

   a). Theft.

   b). Making/selling of illegal substances.

   c). Fraud.

   d). Blackmail.

   d). Kidnap and ransom.

   e). Assassination services.

   f). Specialist services.

Brian and Joan don't like any of the options, but as necessity pushes them to make decisions, the high-risk choices they make ultimately creates fear, stress, adventure, fun and ....? Enjoy the story.

I would like to thank Christine Bell, Karen Rutter and Ken Smith Esq. for their help with editing and supportive commentary. If any future reader finds any grammatical errors or consider the book to be boring or disappointing, it is my intention to entirely blame them! Oh! One more thing, no animals were hurt in the writing of this book.

Thanks for all your help Christine.

John.

Copyright ©2020 John Lamb

All rights reserved. No part of this book may be reproduced, stored in a retrieval system or transmitted in any form or by any means without the prior written permission of the publishers, except by a reviewer who may quote brief passages in a review to be printed by a newspaper, magazine or journal.

CHAPTER 1.

THE CLOCK 'TICKED AND TOCKED' monotonously on the mantle shelf, it was one of those expensive, ornamental faced timepieces set in an elaborate brass case with a decorative glass fronted door that allowed the pendulum, which was responsible for the irritating sound, to be viewed. Pictures, china trinkets and gilded ornaments adorned the marble surround to the fire burning in the hearth, where the coals crackled and moved in the grate, causing the flames to lick up the chimney and send a wave of heat across the room.

The warmth touched the skin on my neck; the only skin currently exposed since my head was covered by a balaclava my wife Joan had knitted. It had been skilfully made to fit my face; the eye, nostril and mouth holes were all perfectly positioned. She had made a matching one for herself; there wasn't many couples who could claim to possess 'His and Her' balaclavas! She had also knitted matching woollen gloves, but we'd both found these a little cumbersome, especially when there was a need to tie knots or perform other intricate tasks; they didn't easily allow access to perform the necessary and regular personal lavatory visits that on occasions such as tonight, were all too frequent. Now we both had to wear plastic 'surgical' gloves, which caused an itchy rash between my fingers that needed constant rubbing to relieve the irritation.

The fire cast a shadowy glow across the room, its flickering light was supported by two lamps, which stood behind each of the two large armchairs at either side of the fire. The warmth and the comfort of my armchair was a soporific combination, and when added to the fact that it was well past my normal bedtime, I'd begun to doze. The thoughts of how and why I came to be sitting here drifted dreamily into my mind.

I was jarred back to full wakefulness as the infuriating clock chimed loudly to signal 11 o'clock. Joan had been away for almost an hour and I began to worry about her, it shouldn't be taking this long, unless there was a problem. I glanced across at the other armchair where my hostage, Mr Armstrong sat, his ankles and wrists were bound quite tightly to prevent him leaving the chair. His face was covered by a linen sack, which again had been made by Joan out of an old pillowcase and now had the benefit of draw strings at the open end so it could be conveniently tightened under the chin. Mr Armstrong had initially complained bitterly that his restraints were too tight and he couldn't breathe very well with the sack over his head, so I had loosened things off a bit, trying to make him as comfortable as possible; the man had finally settled quietly to his fate.

I had thought about explaining to Mr Armstrong why Joan and I were doing this, perhaps in an effort to secure his sympathy and understanding, but we had agreed not to get personally involved with our 'victims' and any spoken words must be kept to a minimum. I was therefore left with only my thoughts to pass the time, reflecting on my failings and how our lives had been driven to this moment.

I know I wasn't entirely to blame for our current situation; Joan and I had always made major decisions throughout our married life together, but nevertheless, in this instance I did blame myself, I should have known better. I knew our decision was driven by greed, we should've been content with what we had, but when a fantastic 'once in a lifetime' opportunity had been offered, we found the temptation too irresistible.

It had all started when we approached the time for our retirement. Joan had worked most of her adult life as an accounts clerk in a pharmaceutical company office, her wage had never been huge, but she had always put aside some of her money into the company pension scheme. I had been in the printing industry since leaving school, a good, steady career that had provided for the family needs, but never achieving any high-level position. I think we considered ourselves as being very ordinary, steady, down to earth, sensible people.

We had been considering our options of how to choose a pension provider and had been quite overwhelmed by the volume of information and quotations presented to us; we were left thoroughly confused and incapable of deciding what we should do. When a smart, professional young man arrived at our door and introduced himself as an executive of an international, privately operated investment fund, who had been recommended by 'a mutual acquaintance' to contact us and present an exciting pension proposal that had already benefitted many retired people like ourselves, we were quite interested. He offered us an opportunity to benefit from ongoing projects that would not only generate tremendous income returns, but since they were derived from substantial property based investments, we could be certain both our income and capital would be protected with a 'cast iron', inflation proof return, supported by an insurance backed guarantee. It seemed like divine intervention and the answer to our prayers. We never felt pressurised, he gave us plenty of time to consider his proposals; everything was so well presented, the glossy literature, the website and all the online details illustrating the projects and the investment company. The profitable, secure returns on offer all reassured and promised us everything we had wanted and much, much more for our retirement.

Looking back I cannot believe we were so gullible, but since the opportunity 'guaranteed' to more than double the best projected pension returns we'd been offered, and would allow us to afford a comfortable existence, with spare cash for holidays and treats for the family, so much better than our original expectation of 'just scraping by', we couldn't resist the offer and signed over our money; it was an opportunity too good to miss.

As we approached our retirement dates, we contacted the company to arrange for our pension payments to commence. We heard nothing. After months of futile efforts to locate where our investments had gone, we realised we had been duped, and nobody could help us. We both still find it hard to talk about; that hollow, empty feeling that was only relieved and filled with emotions of anger and rage. How could someone do this to us? The tears of frustration and bitterness as we realised we could no longer afford to maintain our current lifestyle for more than a few months with what little money we had left.

To rationalise our plight, I was prompted to write a letter to both myself and Joan summarising our situation and setting out our options. The letter read: -

"Dear Mr and Mrs Collins,

I am sorry to hear of the recent 'disappearance' of your pension funds and entire life savings, you obviously must feel much aggrieved that fate has dealt you such a terrible blow. However, the moment has come for you both to carefully consider the options now available, so you may 'live' with your new-found financial challenges. After much consideration, I believe these options can be summarised as follows: -

1). Live within your means: - I understand this requires you to live entirely on your state pension, which is very little. You would have to leave your current house, since the rent you pay is almost double the amount of these pension receipts and go onto a housing waiting list. If you're lucky you will be offered a small one bedroomed flat, probably in one of those local tower blocks where being offered drugs and threatened with violence and theft on a regular basis will be something you'll have to grow accustomed to.

There will be no treats, no Christmas presents for the family, no holidays, it will be just one long miserable and frugal existence, putting money aside for the rent, gas, electric and TV, with whatever meagre sum is left being split between essential groceries and clothes. You may however, be able to make some new friends down at the foodbank or when you're queuing at the housing benefits office.

2). Suicide: - This option has several benefits. You will not have to leave your current house immediately or search for a new, less expensive alternative. Life can carry on as normal until the last few days before your money runs out, giving you plenty of time to arrange everything for an organised and controlled 'departure'. The family will probably be a bit shocked, but at least you won't have to worry about the indignity of admitting your failure to them or having to accept their charitable help while living in miserable poverty.

3). Continue working: - Having now retired it may be difficult to resurrect careers that would generate incomes to compare with what you earned before your retirement. However, this would only stave off the inevitable since neither of you could work for very much longer anyway, particularly you Mr Collins with your anxiety issues, bad back and asthma, but you also Mrs Collins with your angina and arthritic hip. Both of you know perfectly well that you lack any motivation to re-enter the job market and recommence work, so I believe this would be a difficult option, but not impossible.

4) Other means of income generation: - These can be placed under two sub-headings – Legal and Illegal.

Legal: -

a). Put all your remaining money either as a bet on a horse or to buy lottery tickets. This could achieve the result you want by replacing your pension fund in one big win, or, as is more likely, to end in a rapid loss that exacerbates further your critical situation.

b). Start your own business. Again, much like gambling, unless the business is an instant overnight success with clients/customers queuing at the door to buy your products or services, any project is probably not going to help in the time you have available before your final savings run out, even assuming the business didn't require you to invest any money to get it started in the first place. There is also the problem, as I understand, that you have no idea what business you could start and no experience of running a business.

Illegal: -

There are several areas of crime to consider and I have noted these below. Obviously there are many sub-categories that you can add yourself for further consideration and in more detail at a later time: -

a). Theft.

b). Making or selling illegal substances.

c). Fraud.

d). Blackmail.

d). Kidnap and ransom.

e). Assassination services.

f). Specialist services.

The upside of illegal activities are that they can bring instant and potentially substantial financial reward, and even if you are apprehended at least you will be provided with free board and lodgings! Secondly, you are both quite elderly and not in the greatest of health and will therefore appear, in most circumstances, to be innocent and above suspicion as you don't fit the profile of criminals; who could ever suspect two geriatrics like yourselves of being involved in anything illegal, particularly since neither of you have any criminal record; you've never even had a parking ticket!

My advice would be to start small, learn quick and think big.

Yours sincerely.

I know I wrote this letter to ourselves, which did seem a bit foolish at the time, but it clearly set out our situation and has been a great help in focussing and stimulating our thoughts for the forthcoming crucial discussions. It's helped us to 'move on' from the bitter, paralysed inertia that we had fallen into after the realisation of our financial loss and our current dire situation.

CHAPTER 2.

IT WAS EARLY ONE SUNDAY MORNING, a morning that promised to be a lovely spring day as we sat at our kitchen table looking out of the patio window to the garden where clumps of daffodils and crocuses gave some brightness to the winter colours. Joan had made us a large mug of instant coffee that was used to wash down the soft, warm buttered toast laid before us for breakfast. I took Joan's hand and squeezed it to show my thanks and to give support for the difficult conversation we planned to have. Everything was set out on the table – paper, pencils, pens, coloured pencils and a ruler in case we needed to draw a chart, a calculator, rubber, paper clips and Tippex. We were ready to do something. Our efforts to prepare things, including ourselves, had taken weeks, but we found clinging to our inertia and doing nothing so much easier than facing our anxiety and fears and actually doing something.

The coffee was drank, the toast was eaten and still our paper, pencils and equipment lay unused, our silent and the much-extended moment of looking out of the window at the spring scene was becoming awkward. I noticed Joan had started chewing her nails; she'd always loved having long painted nails, but now they were short and plain and unpainted. She had become a sad person, not who she really was, she was just 'sad', and depressed, and worried, and frightened, and she hadn't put any makeup on or the usual bright lipstick that she liked. She had suddenly started to look old. Her demeanour made me want to weep, she deserved so much more than this, I needed to be stronger, so I finally picked up my copy of the letter we'd written to ourselves, with a determination I didn't feel.

"I think the best way to start is for us to go through each of the points and break them into those things we can't or won't do, those things that need more thought, and those we could do." Joan sat up in her chair, still with little enthusiasm and simply nodded before taking three pieces of paper and a pen. At the top of the first page she wrote: -

VERY, VERY SHITTY IDEAS.

On the second: -

VERY SHITTY IDEAS.

And on the third: -

SHITTY IDEAS.

She looked up at me with a 'smile', the entire foolishness of our situation and the decisions we must make seemed to be summarised in the titles written on those three sheets of paper and the image of Joan's idiotic smile. We stared at each other before unexpectedly bursting out in hysterical laughter, something neither of us had done in a while and it seemed to release much of the tension that had controlled our lives for too long.

As we began to calm, still chuckling as we wiped the laughter tears from our eyes, I suggested we talk about 'Living within our means'. Joan immediately turned to page one and wrote this idea down.

"Why?" I asked.

"Because that's not who we are. We've always lived our lives to the full and tried hard to make sure we had fun and enjoyed ourselves. As we wrote down in the letter, this will just ensure the rest of our lives will be spent in miserable poverty, so it is, in my opinion, a VERY, VERY SHITTY idea. What do you think?"

"I agree, I can't ever imagine us living like that. I also can't imagine us committing, well you know, ending it all, so should we put that under the same heading?"

"No, I know we've both thought about this as a way out and we should talk about it, but perhaps not yet, let's work through all the other ideas, it should only be our 'final' solution when everything else has failed." Joan suggested, trying to avoid the topic herself.

"You're right, we've obviously both thought about …," I paused, again finding it difficult to use the word, "so we should talk, and I suppose if we're going to, it should be now, since it's on our minds and before we get distracted. We must be prepared, by having a plan agreed detailing the how, where and under what circumstances this becomes the right choice. I suggest this for two reasons; the first is in case we must act quickly, and secondly because we cannot keep avoiding the thought or mentioning the word, 'suicide'. We need to fully appreciate the details and implications so we can move on." I spluttered.

"Bloody hell Brian, you make it sound like a military exercise!"

"And like everything we're thinking of doing we must be organised and prepared," I continued, trying to sound convincing and in control. "We need a fourth sheet of paper with a heading – 'WHEN ALL ELSE FAILS' and the first item on that list should be 'SUICIDE'." Joan obliged and continued to look at the new page, her pen poised, thinking, before writing another line with the word HOW as a subheading.

"Any ideas?" she asked.

"How about slitting our wrists, or hanging, drowning or electrocution?" I asked, warming a little more to the topic.

"No." she replied. "It must be painless, and those methods would be really messy and unpleasant for whoever had to clear us away. I was thinking more along the lines of an overdose, sleeping pills type of stuff, so we could be comfortable in bed together, laid out ready to go in a coffin." She ended with a grimace.

"The question is, could we get enough of the right drug to be certain we wouldn't survive, there's no point in taking something, sleeping for two days, and then waking up hungry and thirsty! I don't suppose you could buy anything from the chemist that would be strong enough; I've never heard of anyone dying from an overdose of Night-Nurse type of stuff. I agree with the concept of a 'pain free', 'tidy' death, but neither of us have any experience of what to take and I can't think of who we could ask, if there is even anyone we could ask without raising eyebrows."

We sat silently thinking about who we could consult on how to kill ourselves with no pain and without making a mess. After some thought I reconsidered.

"I don't think getting sleeping pills would be difficult, I could go to my doctor, you go to yours and we both get some sleeping pills each. I'll make appointments straightaway." I decided. "If the doctor only prescribes something very mild, we can always go back in a couple of weeks' and ask for something stronger."

"You're right, we do need to have this carefully worked out while we have cool heads," proclaimed Joan, "trying to arrange things under pressure could only end with a quick drive to the cliff at Beachy Head!"

"I never considered jumping off a cliff and I don't know if I could." I thought aloud. "We need to think some more about the 'how' over the next few days, but we also need to consider the other practicalities – Do we leave a note for the family and what do we say? Do we make plans for the funeral? Who should be invited? What hymns we want sung? What catering arrangement would we like? Should there be a free bar? Do we want to be buried or cremated? Fucking hell Joan, this is all too complicated, I can feel a panic attack coming on just trying to plan our deaths, I'm beginning to think that living may be easier to plan."

"I agree, it's not something we should rush to decide in a few hours, let's leave the suicide arrangements for now and continue, we can complete them in detail over the next week or so, hopefully we won't need them in a hurry. Let's move on, what's next?"

"That would be the CONTINUE WORKING option," I groaned, "perhaps talking about suicide may be more interesting!"

"The thought of going back to working in an office again fills me with dread," commented Joan, "spending more time listening to the constant whining and complaining of people and their small minded, boring lives, the same things week in and week out for me is not an option, so I'll put this under VERY SHITTY IDEAS on page two, in case we have no choice. Let's move on."

"OK, the next item is OTHER MEANS OF INCOME GENERATION. Firstly, the LEGAL options. I love the boldness of the high stakes gambling idea, imagine the feeling of having put all your money on a single bet; the anxiety, tension and excitement of watching your horse running with your whole life dependent on it winning. How would you feel if it won?"

"I get goose bumps just thinking about the idea, your imagination can run wild. The problem is I can also imagine our complete devastation if we lost, all our hopes and dreams would be crushed in an instant. We would certainly feel like embracing a suicide pack if that were to happen, we'd need to finish the suicide discussion and complete our 'exit' plans before we back a horse. This can go on page three – SHITTY IDEAS." I nodded my agreement. "What about buying thousands of lottery tickets?" continued Joan.

"My issues with buying lottery tickets are the time it would take to buy 'thousands' of tickets, then checking them and finally claiming the dozens of small wins and free-play tickets, it would be like 'dying by a thousand cuts' and could take forever to lose, which I'm sure will be the final outcome. The likelihood of winning a substantial amount are statistically not good, but I suppose you never know, someone's got to win, it certainly would keep us occupied and our hopes alive for quite a time." I suggested without much enthusiasm. "Should we put that on the SHITTY IDEAS list as well?" Joan paused before agreeing with a simple "OK" that was quietly spoken with a tinge of disappointment; she'd obviously thought this was a good idea. She looked over at the letter to see what was next.

"I don't think we should even talk about 'STARTING OUR OWN BUSINESS', it's just a non-starter. We've no ideas what type of business we could run, or how to run a business, or prepare a business plan, or attract customers for sales, never mind having sufficient capital to start something, so I'm just going to put this straight onto the VERY VERY SHITTY IDEAS list." She paused before reflecting on our progress.

"We've not made many positive decisions so far, which is disappointing. I suggest we open a bottle of wine and start drinking. Don't raise your eyebrows Brian," Joan rebuked accusingly, "I know it's just after ten o'clock but what the hell, it's not going to kill us, more's the pity!" She laughed as she went to the cupboard, selected a bottle of red wine and started opening it while I took two glasses off the shelf.

"Cheers," we toasted. "Here's to developing better and more prosperous idea's under the ILLEGAL options, since there seems to be few LEGAL opportunities we like. I always felt a great deal more enthusiasm for considering these, probably because neither of us ever contemplated them as being any more that imaginings, never something we would seriously consider doing, but now I think we have to look at these more extreme ideas as real options."

"I can't believe I'm agreeing with you, they do make me smile when I imagine us wearing stripped shirts and Lone Ranger type masks while committing bank robberies and jewellery heists, hobbling away with a hoard of stuff slung over our shoulders in sacks clearly marked as SWAG." We both laughed as we visualised the image Joan had created of two geriatrics fleeing from the scene of a robbery using Zimmer frames as getaway vehicles, looking like cartoon figures. I sensed the wine was already beginning to help with our creative thinking!

"I know we put THEFT on our list and we just laughed at the thought of us trying to rob a bank or jewellery shop, but I just can't think of any type of robbery we would be capable of," exclaimed Joan.

"What about burglary? With some planning and by choosing the right property I'm sure we can break into a house and steal some stuff." I suggested.

"You're forgetting that we're not professional thieves, how could we get rid of the 'stuff' we stole? What we want is cash only, not tv's and computer type 'stuff', or even jewellery. We wouldn't have a clue how to find a 'Fence', if that's the correct name for such a person!"

"Good point, I was getting carried away again and you're right, it is only cash we really want to steal. I can't think of what or who we could rob; neither of us are capable of mugging someone unless they were really old and disabled, and even then, we might come off worst! It's also likely that the amount we could steal from them probably wouldn't be much anyway, and I think morally the concept of robbing the poor to feed the poor is not right"

We sat quietly for several minutes, drinking the wine as we tried to think of any other suggestions. It soon became obvious that THEFT should be placed on the SHITTY IDEAS list since we still believed there was a possibility something could work; we just hadn't thought of it.

Onto the VERY VERY SHITTY list went Making/selling illegal substances despite laughing as we recalled the series on TV, Breaking Bad, when Walter White, a chemistry teacher, discovers that he has cancer and decides to get into the meth-making business to repay his medical debts. Definitely not something we could ever contemplate, but amusing, nevertheless.

FRAUD was the next item on the list, and we talked at length of different potential ideas. The obvious one was trying to replicate the pension style scam that we'd lost all of our money to. The trouble was that the people who had defrauded us had been so professional, with their brochures and website showing photos of investment properties let to reputable, well known tenants that ensured a secure and reliable income; graphs and charts that illustrated how the income and therefore our pensions would grow; business cards and references in abundance. We realised we could never compete. Unfortunately now, having had the discussion and raised the issue once again, the feelings of bitter anger, shame and disappointment descended on us both like a black cloud. Joan opened another bottle of wine.

We decided to put FRAUD onto the VERY VERY SHITTY list. I finally broke our silence by suggesting, as positively as I could and in an effort to restart our discussions.

"I think BLACKMAIL, the next idea on the list offers us more opportunity."

"How the hell could you possibly think our situation could improve and offer us more opportunities if we became blackmailers?" Joan demanded with a very slight slur. I was thinking we should have something to eat, but Joan seemed to be on a mission as she filled our glasses again, finishing the bottle.

"Well, everyone does things at some point in their lives that they don't want their wife or husband or employer to know about."

"Do you have personal experience of this Brian, have you done things that you didn't want me to know about?"

"Joan, this is not about what I have done or you for that matter." I felt a little defensive as she stared at me, I tried to deflect the question, I hoped she couldn't see the memories that flashed through my mind as I spoke. "I'm trying to make a general statement that we should be able to discover something about an old colleague or even a neighbour or friend who has done or is doing something we could blackmail them with."

"I know Evie Johnson is certain her husband is having an affair with one of his shop assistants." Joan suggested.

"Really! You mean Andrew Johnson, the pharmacist?" Joan nodded confidently. "Andrew is having an affair with one of the women who works in his shop. How did you find this out?"

"Evie told me that she'd seen them driving away from the shop together in his car. When he got home later and she asked where he'd been, he told her he'd had a Bowls Club meeting, he never mentioned driving away with a 'Tart in his car', as Evie described the incident."

"Joan, this is brilliant, I told you this was a good idea, it can be our first 'mission'."

"Well, I think before we go out to buy deerstalker hats and Meerschaum pipes, I'll make us something to eat, I think I must be getting a bit pissed because you're beginning to look quite sexy!" she laughed.

"Shit! let me help cut the bread, best to get us both sobered up, we don't want to do anything 'messy'. I can't ever remember drinking two bottles of wine before 11.00 in the morning!"

"We did once," Joan smiled at a memory as she spread some pickles on top of the bread, pausing with a slice of corned beef held between her fingers, "when we were on holiday in Spain and my mother had taken the children off early one day on a boat trip. We had sex twice and drank two bottles of wine and were dressed and down to the restaurant before midday to have lunch." The corner of the corn beef slice had drooped down in a curve and finally broke off, falling onto the bread at an odd angle but distracted Joan from her memory as she continued to prepare the sandwiches.

"There was also that time our early morning flight was cancelled when we were due to fly back from Yugoslavia. We went to that little taverna on the seafront with our suitcases to book in for the night, but it was too early and they weren't properly open so we bought some wine and sat and drank it on the beach in the sunshine. Do you remember, we fell asleep and woke up a few hours later and our faces and arms were burnt bright red." We laughed at this memory and with the rather makeshift sandwiches we sat and began eating them with some crisps. This had become a very strange morning, but I was determined that we would continue, we were starting to make some progress with our plans.

I was first to finish so I put the kettle on to make some coffee. "BLACKMAIL definitely must go on the SHITTY LIST and we must add a few notes on getting some evidence to blackmail the philandering chemist, he's quite wealthy and I've never really liked him; he always seems to think he's better than everyone else. Just a thought, as part of our financial demands we could get him to give us some strong sleeping tablets! Can you think of anyone else that's up to no good?"

"Not immediately, but I'm sure once we start looking, we'll find things about other people, particularly if I start getting my hair done at the salon every week, I'll get all the gossip there!"

"I can't think of anybody offhand either, but I do have a few thoughts. OK, let's leave BLACKMAIL for now and try KIDNAP AND RANSOM. I have a great idea for this. Instead of kidnapping a person or child, which neither of us could do, we 'kidnap' people's pets. We rename this section PETNAP AND RANSOM. A lot of these cutie furballs are treated like babies and are loved by their owners more than anything in the world, they'd pay a fortune to get them back. How hard could it be to take someone's little pet when they're not looking. Even if we get caught it would be easy to come up with an excuse like, 'I thought it was ours'. What do you think?" I asked, looking at Joan who appeared extremely attentive and was nodding with a supportive smile on her face.

"I really like that idea, it's simple and as you say, kidnapping the animal shouldn't be difficult. Have you thought about what we do after we've got it; how do we know who to contact if it has one of those 'chips'? When we've got the owner's name, how do we contact them to demand the money? How do we give the dog back?" Joan could see that I'd turned on my computer and she waited while I tapped on the keyboard with my one fingered style, constantly glancing between the keyboard and the screen.

"I love watching as you work on the computer, the concentration on your crinkly face and how your pointy nose seems to peck when your head bobs up and down as you type reminds me.." I stopped typing and gave her a sour look, which she ignored when I started typing again, concentrating on trying to stop my head from 'bobbing'. Joan continued as if I hadn't interrupted her. "It reminds me of your nickname when we first met, that was before I later discovered, most pleasurably I should add, that there was a much more impressive reason for you to be called the 'Woodpecker'!" I again stopped typing and looked at her and she smiled back; her memories had reminded me that we'd been together for a very long time, we had history, and the thought we would always be together, no matter what happened, gave me a warm feeling. I returned her smile and leant over to kiss her to show my love and forgiveness for her comments. As we parted I returned to my typing. Joan was quiet, she was obviously thinking about something and suddenly surprised me with her explanation.

"In an odd sort of way I'm beginning to enjoy this bizarre challenge and the creative ideas and solutions we're considering, I find it quite uplifting and energizing, it feels like a new adventure for us both and I can't wait to start becoming a proper criminal!" I laughed at her enthusiasm, feeling a similar energy myself for our new opportunities. I returned to my internet searches, focusing once again on finding answers to her questions to help us progress with our petnapping plans.

"This is interesting." I said, again turning to face Joan and catching her smiling to herself; I wondered what she could possibly be thinking about that would make her smile given the seriousness of our current plan to kidnap and ransom someone's much loved pet, but I made no comment. "We can buy a microchip scanner online and it'll give us the owner's contact details when you scan the dog. It costs £159.99; could be a good investment and does answer your first question. Once we've got the details, I think it would be best to telephone the owner from a telephone box or a 'pay as you go' phone so the call can't be traced…. hold that thought." My attention returned to the computer and after a few more minutes I had the information I was looking for. "We telephone the owner using a voice changer, you can buy one from the Spy Shop for only £65.75 and then, even if it's a friend or neighbour's pet they'll not recognise us. We can demand they leave the cash in a safe place for us to collect and the dog can be tied up somewhere for them to collect. Simple, quick money."

We both sat in silence before Joan picked up her papers and on another new sheet she wrote – GOOD IDEAS and underneath she wrote PETNAP AND RANSOM and continued to write out all I'd suggested, adding additional refinements of her own, particularly with regards to having the money delivered and the dog released. She also crossed off BLACKMAIL from the SHITTY LIST and put it on the GOOD IDEAS list as well, again with a few notes of the individual plan.

"I can't wait, I've always hated those selfish, snooty bastards who care more for their cutie little pets than for hungry children, I'll find it quite hard to only take the money without killing the horrible little 'rat on a stick' afterwards, but I suppose that wouldn't be good for business!" They both laughed at Joan's inappropriate and politically incorrect comments.

"I know what you mean, I've watched them in the park as they take out their bundle of joy so it can have a shit and a piss where the children play, before running around sniffing other dog's arses and excrement, then giving their own arse a good lick and returning happily to their proud owners who hold them up so they can lick and kiss their faces. I cringe at the thought of how they disgust me. I think this is my favourite idea so far and the next idea may allow you to have your wishes granted. Any thoughts on ASSASSINATION SERVICES?"

"I have no idea what we originally had in mind when we put 'assassination services' in the letter, but I could never kill anyone, promise me no matter how much money is involved we won't kill anyone." Joan demanded.

"Are you sure? would you kill a child abuser for £20000?" I asked.

"No, that's for the authorities to deal with."

"£50000?"

Joan paused, just for a second too long before again saying "No".

"What about if he's beating his wife and raping his 10-year-old daughter and they wouldn't report it to the authorities because they were frightened of him?"

"Well, OK, under those circumstances and I had the means and opportunity I would kill him, probably for nothing!"

"So, you would kill someone." I teased.

"That's not the point," Joan protested, "we're never going to be aware of this type of person and we'll never be in a situation where we could kill someone, so it's all academic."

"I know, I was only joking. I cannot remember why we wrote this down either; I can only think we wanted as many options as we could think of to make some money. However, it could link into the next idea, which was SPECIALIST SERVICES. Could we assassinate 'pesky pets?"

"You mean like the neighbour's dogs that constantly bark, or their cats that come into the garden and shit in the flower bed, like our neighbour's, the Maxwell's pets do. Yes, I could pay to have them assassinated!"

"You mean assassinate the pets, not the Maxwells?" I laughed.

"I get so angry sometimes I feel it would be great to get rid of them all, but no, just the pets. The problem with this idea is how to market the service; you can't really put an advert in the local paper offering *'to rid the neighbourhood of annoying pets – a unique service at low cost'*. I know people complain but I imagine there would be few, if any, who could bring themselves to pay for their neighbours' pets to be killed. I love the idea, but don't think it's a money maker." Joan advised, with a look that suggested she held some hope that I would disagree and explain a plan to prove otherwise. But I couldn't. As there was no means of developing what both us felt was a good idea, we agreed it should be dropped.

"The only other idea I had, and I should've raised it earlier as it's perfectly legal, is to start a Private Detective Agency, particularly as a cover and support to the two GOOD IDEAS we have on our list."

"I agree," Joan interrupted, "we could get paid by a client to spy and then earn an extra bonus by blackmailing the person we've been employed to spy on." I nodded and smiled in admiration at how quickly Joan had developed a criminal mind.

We sat quietly for some moments having reached the end of the suggestions written in 'the letter'. I broke the silence by suggesting we review what we'd agreed.

"We seem to have three GOOD IDEAS: -

1). Private Detective Agency work.

2). Blackmail.

3). Pet kidnapping.

I think all the others..."

"I've just had another good idea," interrupted Joan enthusiastically, "it would be under the title of THEFT, which we originally put on the SHITTY LIST, but I've thought of a twist." She paused, appearing to work through her new plan in her mind. As the seconds turned into minutes, I saw her look of concentration change as a smile began to crease her face.

"I think you'll like this plan," she chuckled, "I've nearly got it worked out, but it needs more detail. Firstly, we select a house of a 'mature', wealthy couple with no other occupants living in the property. On an evening we approach the house with a small empty box, put on masks so we can't be identified, and both have an imitation gun concealed in our hand. We put the box at the front door and ring the bell, stepping to the side of the door so we can't be immediately seen. When the door is opened our prey sees the box and bends to pick it up, believing it's simply been left by a courier or someone. While they're distracted, we push them into the hall, threaten them with our guns, shut the front door and march them into the sitting room, put blindfolds over their heads and tie them to chairs."

"We then explain that we don't want to hurt them, but we will if they don't do exactly what we tell them to do, which is firstly to sit in silence until 10.45pm when the woman will be untied and her blindfold removed. She will, after we threaten to shoot her husband in the foot, collect up all her and her husband's credit and bank cards, ensuring she has all the necessary codes. I leave with her in their car and drive to the nearest cash point machine where she withdraws the maximum amount of cash from each card. We then return, she gets tied up and blindfolded again until 12.30 am when she and I repeat the cashpoint visit. After once again returning, retying and blindfolding her we leave with what will hopefully be a lot of cash. What do you think?" Joan appeared incredibly pleased with herself.

"Joan, you never cease to amaze me, that is brilliant, the only thing I don't understand is why make a withdrawal at 10.45 pm and then again at 12.30am?"

"That's because I know you can only take out a certain amount of money from a cashpoint machine in a day and that's why I suggest these times to ensure the withdrawals are spread across two separate days." Joan explained smugly.

"Very clever, and I won't ask how you know this. I can't immediately find fault with your plan and it definitely goes on the GOOD IDEAS list so we can work through the details later. Any other bright ideas? I can't think of any and would suggest we chuck away all the SHITTY lists and just focus on our four good ideas. Also, if you move 'Betting on a horse' and 'buying lottery tickets' onto the 'WHEN ALL ELSE FAILS LIST, that tidies everything up."

"I have one immediate suggestion," Joan smiled, " I think you should pour us a large gin and tonic to celebrate, I feel we deserve it, we've both changed from being seriously depressed first thing this morning, to becoming enthusiastic and quite optimistic about our future, it's certainly feels like a good start to us making our fortune in a life of crime. Who knows how it'll all work out."

CHAPTER 3.

THE NEXT MORNING neither of us felt like the mastermind crime duo that we had been when we went to bed. A mixture of too much alcohol, too little food and an over exerted imagination had ruined our sleep. We now sat at the kitchen table once again, this time sipping a cup of coffee, neither of us wanting to eat any of the Greek yoghurt, fruit and honey that Joan had put out for breakfast, including her 'special' packet of exotic seeds that must be sprinkled over, 'to keep us regular', as an extra benefit; I always felt this was a very disappointing breakfast, preferring bacon, egg, sausage, black pudding and baked beans 'to keep me regular' as an alternative.

This morning however, I felt extremely jaded; the restless and uneasy night's sleep, caused by my mind plotting and planning burglaries, highjacks, car thefts, kidnappings, dead cats strung up from lampposts and little pet dogs disguised as babies being pushed away in prams while their owners ran around in a panic searching fruitlessly for their little darlings. All these dreams, thoughts and plans had felt so simple, practical and successful in those half wakeful moments during the night. Unfortunately, in the grim light of day they seemed foolish and impractical.

Again, we found ourselves sitting looking out over the garden; it was raining this morning, so the daffodils and crocuses seemed to hang limp as they tried to support the clinging raindrops. Again, the silence drifted along and as my mind cleared, I began to reflect on our efforts from the previous day; some of the ideas and suggestions we discussed will always remain in my memory. I also began to realise for the first time in many months, and despite the hangover, I felt quite excited, even exhilarated at embarking on a life filled with new challenges, even though they were nearly all completely illegal and immoral.

My gaze turned away from the drooping daffodils and limp crocuses to see that Joan was staring at me with a huge grin on her face.

"I've just amused myself while you were away in dreamland, by looking through the four plans we wrote down. Surprisingly, despite all the booze, they still sound very plausible this morning. I know I said it yesterday but I've got to say it again, I can't wait to get started spying, stealing, kidnapping and blackmailing, I wish we'd packed in our jobs and started doing this years ago!" We both laughed together, her enthusiastic energy instantly drove away any fears or doubts I may have woken up with along with my headache, which had also miraculously disappeared.

"Who are you and what have you done with my wife?" I asked laughing at her sparkling eyes and mischievous grin.

"She's gone, left, never to return and has been replaced by me and from henceforth I will be known by you and the criminal fraternity as 'Farc' and you will be called 'Woody'."

"Eh?" I exclaimed, "Woody I understand but 'Farc', what sort of a criminal name is that?"

"It was my nickname at school, because of my first name." Explained Joan and was about to explain further as to the meaning when it suddenly dawned on me.

"I get it now, Joan Farc. Is that what you used to be called at school, you never told me that."

"That's because as we got into teenage years and boys began to snigger and ask if I was a 'Good Farc' I insisted that all my friends called me Joan."

"OK, from now on I'll call you Farc, but only when we're out on our criminal activities," I chuckled, Joan was constantly surprising me with revelations like this and so many different characteristics of herself that I didn't know or hadn't seen before; I marvelled at her determination and enthusiasm, she gave me so much strength, I wanted to hold her and tell her how much I loved her, just for being her.

CHAPTER 4.

I AWOKE WITH A START, completely confused. In my dream state I thought I was in my own bed next to Joan, we were warm and comfortable and holding each other, but as my senses cleared I realised I'd been woken by Mr. Armstrong who had groaned loudly as he'd pulled against his bindings and the stuffy sack that was still tied over his head. I did feel sorry for him, he was obviously struggling to find a comfortable position as he dozed uncomfortably.

I felt so tired. I couldn't understand why it was such a constant struggle to stop myself from falling into a very deep sleep. I looked at the clock, it was nearly eleven- thirty. Where was Joan? What was taking her so long? I hoped she was alright. The fire was so warm, the chair so comfortable and the clock continued to tick slowly like a soporific metronome. Mr. Armstrong seemed to have stopped writhing against his restraints and had settled again. My mind returned to recalling those earlier times when Joan and I developed our newly discovered retirement options.

CHAPTER 5.

OUR FIRST ACTION was to have printed up some business cards for our 'Private Investigator' enterprise; the bold black ink words on the pure white card gave a classy, professional appearance and simply stated – *BRIAN AND JOAN COLLINS – PRIVATE INVESTIGATORS – DISCRESSION ASSURED*. It then gave our address and telephone numbers. All this information was genuine, something we debated at length before deciding it must be this way given that it was primarily a 'cover' and we would only use them at those times when we needed to explain why we were 'lurking' in odd places, and of course, if we were ever asked for more details of what we were doing we could simply hide behind the 'Client Confidentiality' ruse.

Our first mission was to investigate further the exploits of Andrew Johnson the Pharmacist. It took us a few days of sitting on benches, drinking teas and coffees in the café, walking up and down the high street repeatedly looking in the same shop windows, all so we may watch Andrew Johnson, who never did anything wrong and only observed him performing normal duties in his shop. This was an exhausting, boring and fruitless regime and we realised that the only time he was likely to do anything 'inappropriate' was after the shop closed. We therefore began to park our car close to where he parked his so we may observe who he left with. For the first two evenings he left alone, walked to his car and drove home. We were not very good at 'tailing' him and found it difficult to keep up through the traffic; he always seemed to be lucky, whereas we constantly had to stop to let people cross the road or the traffic lights would change to red just as we approached, after Andrew had passed through. If we hadn't known where he lived, we would've lost him.

After work on the third day, Andrew left the shop, walked to his car and we followed as he drove off, believing he was again about to drive straight home, but after a while his route deviated and he pulled into a car park at the rear of a pub on the edge of town. We followed him in and parked in a vacant space in the corner and watched as he put on his coat and casually walked into the pub. We debated whether we should follow him in and watch what he did and who he met, but decided it was too risky and he was likely to spot us; it would also be impossible to take any incriminating photographs inside anyway. Unfortunately, or fortunately as it turned out, after half an hour I needed to go to the toilet; I realised at this moment our shortcomings when it came to any lengthy 'stakeout' and wondered if in the future we needed to plan some sort of 'in car' facilities, or maybe some incontinence pads to get us through.

I had to walk through the bar area, which wasn't too busy and by the time I reached the toilet door I realised that Andrew wasn't there.

After relieving myself, I approached the bar and asked if there were any other public or meeting rooms, thinking that Andrew could well be innocently attending a meeting in an upstairs room. The barmen however shook his head, advising they only had a small event room, but it was currently unavailable as it was being redecorated, and no they didn't have any letting bedrooms in answer to my second question. As we talked I realised that the main entrance into the bar was at the front of the building and I had entered from the rear car park door. Andrew had obviously left his car and exited the bar through this front door. Bugger!

I returned to the car and told Joan what I'd discovered, and we discussed either giving up and going home or continue waiting in the car park; Andrew would at some point in the evening have to return to his car. We decided to wait, agreeing we would learn nothing if we gave up so easily, but compromised by limiting the wait to 2 hours.

At the end of this period and having had the need for a further two visits to the toilet, Andrew had still not returned, but even though we were very hungry, something else we needed to provide for in the future, and missing our home comforts, we both agreed that since we'd waited this long we had to be more patient, so I made another toilet visit and bought some crisps and pork scratchings to keep us going.

Another hour and a half past, cars and people came and went, it was nearly ten o'clock, our normal bedtime and the earlier patience, determination and enthusiasm had long since gone. Darkness had fallen some time earlier, and the car park was now only illuminated by two bright security lights; watching the insects flying around the white lights was our only source of entertainment. We couldn't think of anything else to talk about, we'd made lists of things we wanted to do for our other projects, agreeing the need to plan carefully the small personal necessities that we'd clearly not done this evening.

A car suddenly drove in, its headlights strafing around the car park narrowly missing illuminating us as it maneuvered into a space beside Andrew's car. Andrew was in the passenger seat and I could see that Joan had raised her camera, I was pleased she had retained some focus, I'd almost forgotten why we were sitting there. I could see that the driver was a young blond woman, probably in her early thirties but it was difficult to see until Andrew opened the door and the courtesy light inside the car came on. Andrew leant across to give her a final goodnight kiss, which became more and more passionate as the seconds passed; I could hear the camera as it clicked repeatedly. As soon as they separated Andrew got out of the car and got into his own, waving as the woman drove away.

When they'd both left we continued to sit quietly in the car, Joan scrolled through the photos she'd taken, showing me the best, most of which were a little distorted by the windows of the two cars, but they clearly identified Andrew and his mistress in a compromising situation.

We went home, stopping at the chip shop for two fish suppers, which we devoured around the kitchen table. I looked again at the photos, while Joan sat quietly, she seemed quite sad.

"These are perfect Joan, we can certainly use them to get quite a lot of cash out of the cheating bastard." I rubbed my hands together like Shakespeare's character, Shylock. "How much do you think we can demand?"

"Poor Elsie, I feel so sorry for her, her suspicions were right. I'm torn between telling her, as a friend should, of what he's doing and showing her the pictures. Or blackmailing him. What a dreadful man to betray her like that. Poor Elsie." Joan repeated angrily.

"Joan," I spoke calmly and sympathetically, "I understand your concerns for your friend and through the natural progression of these things she will catch him out sooner or later. But until she does, we must remain detached from our personal feelings and profit from the opportunity we've given ourselves; our needs must come first."

"I know," she agreed, "I just feel I'm betraying her. To answer your question though, I would think we could demand at least £1000 from him for these pictures, but if we can get more incriminating photos we could up the price to," she paused, "I'm thinking as much as £10000, what do you think?"

"Wow," was the only comment I could immediately think of, my figure had been around the £250 and I now felt foolishly unambitious. "That would be incredible. What other photos do you think we could get that would raise the price by that much?" I asked, trying not to rub my hands together again.

"If we had followed Andrew to wherever he met and subsequently went to with the woman, I'm sure we could've got a much greater and incriminating selection. Let's carry on with our 'surveillance' and see what else we can find out. One thing that would be useful is finding out exactly who she is and if she does work in the shop as Elsie suspects."

So we did. Louise Taylor, the 'tart in the car', did work in the shop. Whenever they met they seemed to go through the same routine; Andrew parked his car in the pub cark park, went into the pub, had a gin and tonic, answered his phone, walked out the front door and got into Louise's car and drove off, followed of course by us. The drive was uneventful, Louise wasn't an aggressive driver like Andrew so was easier to follow; I suspect we were also becoming more practiced at 'tailing'.

They pulled up outside a small terraced house in a village, about six miles from the pub. On the first night we only managed to take pictures of them climbing out of the car and going into the front door. Lights went on, and off, and then on again sometime later. Louise closed curtains, never did they both appear together in a window to allow a photo to be taken that would identify where they were, which room they were in and of course, doing something that would illustrate what they were up to.

On the third evening we followed them the routine changed; passions were obviously running high because they'd hardly opened the front door before they were kissing passionately, they were already half undressed as they appeared at the upstairs window, Andrew was all over Louise as she tried to close the curtains. Joan's camera never stopped clicking. We had all the evidence we wanted and left them to enjoy themselves and drove home.

Over the intervening days we planned our campaign; we'd purchased a box of surgical gloves to wear whenever we were preparing 'victim correspondence' and a 'pay as you go phone' that we used to open a new email account; we knew this could be used later for our other endeavors. We printed a selection of pictures that told the passionate story of Andrew and Louise's affair and we also printed a message on simple plain paper with bold black letters which read:-

Dear Mr. Johnson,

We have been watching you and are so pleased you are enjoying the company of Ms. Taylor. We enclose a selection of pictures as mementos of your most recent times spent together, something for you to treasure!

Are you this passionate with your wife? Perhaps we could send her a similar collection of pictures and ask her, but you probably don't want that to happen! To 'persuade' us not to share these and the many other pictures we have with her we must ask you to pay us £10,000, in cash, in 3 days' time.

We would appreciate your agreement to these simple terms by sending us a confirmatory email to mailer.black@.....com after which we will send you clear instructions as to what to do next.

We look forward to hearing from you soon.

Kind regards!

PS. Needless to say, these pictures will be immediately sent to your wife Elsie if you involve any other person or authority. We will continue watching!

Wearing our surgical gloves we put the letter and the selection of photographs into a plain brown envelope, addressed – **FOR THE PERSONAL ATTENTION OF MR ANDREW JOHNSON** – and that evening we delivered it through the letterbox of his chemist shop together with one of several leaflets we had taken from the library earlier in the day asking for support for the RSPCA; we delivered the remaining leaflets to other shops on the street to disguise our primary activity.

We could hardly contain our nervous excitement and decided to drive to where we had finally agreed was the most ideal place for Andrew to leave the cash. We had given a huge amount of thought and planned carefully where and how this would happen, recognising it was the moment we would be at our most vulnerable of being observed and identified. Another visit and a further review would do no harm.

Our criteria for selection of this location had been simple; there were to be no CCTV cameras, very few people about and clear views so we could easily observe Andrew at every stage and any other person who may be watching. It also needed to be a place where no one would question why we were there; even after we collected the money we could always claim that we had simply found it and were on our way to the Police Station to hand it in as lost property.

Our 'Perfect' chosen place was a graveyard, which was quite large and had a secluded corner where a bag of money could be left quite securely behind a specific headstone. We both knew this place very well as it was our local church where we had been married there nearly forty years ago. We never considered ourselves as churchgoers and had only returned over the intervening years for the occasional carol service at Christmas and the christening of our children, but since our decision to make this our 'drop', we had attended the Sunday service twice in the past three weeks, quickly remembering why we hadn't attended more frequently! We couldn't believe how drab the whole charade was; the vicar spoke in a droning monotone voice, the hymns were sung without any passion by the small, unenthusiastic congregation. The fabric of the church itself felt tired of its own existence and certainly did not raise our spirits; we were always left feeling depressed.

Outside, the church sat in the middle of a walled graveyard with only two wrought iron entrance gates; one at each end, which seemed to be always locked, apart from times of service and special events – weddings, funerals, christenings etc. We therefore could not avoid the money drop being on a Sunday morning when the church was open, but we both agreed this was the best time in any case as we could blend into the 'crowds' and have a reason to be there.

It was on a Wednesday night we delivered the letter to Andrew's shop and incredibly we received an email from him on the Thursday lunch time. His words sounded fearful as he promised to pay the money and pleaded with us not to send the pictures to his wife, he wrote that he had "made a mistake" and didn't want her to be hurt. He did ask how certain he could be that we wouldn't ask for more money the following week. When we sent our brief reply we assured him that this was a 'one off' event, explaining that if we were to try such a ploy he would have no choice but to tell his wife himself, recognising that our demands could be endless, this would obviously nullify any chance of 'second helpings'.

We told him the 'drop off' would be on Sunday morning at 9.30 am and would give him details on the Saturday night of the exact location and arrangements. We reminded him that he was being watched and if there were any sign of 'others' being present either before, during or after he left the money, it would not be collected and his wife would immediately receive all the information of his infidelity.

He confirmed his understanding and agreement. On the Saturday evening we emailed him details of the church and attached a small sketch showing the location and details of the gravestone that he was to place the money behind – ironically the stone identified itself as the last burial place of a Robin Cashmore – we also confirmed the time and repeated our instruction regarding the involvement of others.

CHAPTER 6.

THE SUNDAY SERVICE was to start at 10.30 am - Joan and I arrived at 8.00am, parked our car in a prechosen position where we could easily watch all the comings and goings. We then walked around the outside perimeter of the church grounds and the little streets; we checked each parked car and carefully watched every vehicle that drove past, nothing seemed suspicious and all seemed very quiet. We returned to our car and waited. At 9.00 am a warden opened both the gates, so we had a slow walk around the churchyard and again were reassured all was well and returned once more to sit in our car.

We'd brought a flask of coffee and some egg sandwiches, which we ate and drank in silence, we couldn't think of anything to say as we both felt very nervous. Just before 9.30 am, Andrew drove up and parked right outside the front entrance, quickly got out and glanced around before taking a small bag from the boot of his car and strode into the churchyard. I couldn't help but notice how pale and nervous he looked; this was a stressful time for us all! We watched closely for anybody to move, other than Andrew, or anything suspicious as he walked to the corner of the graveyard, returning almost immediately, but now without the bag, to his car and drove away.

As agreed, Joan got out of the car to embark on a 'patrol' of the churchyard and perimeter to observe what, if anything had changed since our earlier tour. I drove off to follow Andrew, which wasn't difficult given how little traffic there was and that I knew, or hoped I knew he was returning home. I breathed a huge sigh of relief when he parked his car in the drive and went into his house, reassured that he had no intention of doubling back to the church to observe who was responsible for making him £10,000 poorer.

I returned to the church and walked over to Joan who was sitting on a bench pretending to read a magazine. We smiled at each other reassuringly before walking into the church and sitting down with the other members of the congregation who had begun to arrive. The church was quite cold, colder than it was outside, which seemed odd, there was also a musty smell of dampness and hymn books; a 'church smell' that I'd always believed was the 'smell' of God when I was a child!

We found it almost impossible to concentrate on the service; the vicars sermon seemed to be targeted at us as he spoke of the evils of wrong doings, concluding with a quotation from Corinthians Chapter 6 Verse 10 - ……*nor thieves nor the greedy nor drunkards nor slanderers nor swindlers will inherit the kingdom of God.* We feared we would be punished for what we had done, either by a fireball from God or the police who we visualized would be outside waiting for us to collect the money.

When the service finally ended and we walked back outside, setting off once again to stroll around the churchyard, casually looking at the occasional gravestone until we reached Robin Cashmore's stone. Joan walked to the rear, acted surprised to see a bag lying there, some amateur dramatics that almost made me laugh with nervous hysterics. She picked it up and pretended to explain to me with more poorly mimed theatrics, pointing to where she had just found the bag. We continued to stroll until we left the church and reached our car, I could hardly breathe and could see that Joan was looking very pale, her face was creased with anxiety, it had felt like the longest walk of our lives. I was fumbling for the car keys when a voice from behind shouted.

"Excuse me." We both spun around, fearing the worst. "I couldn't help noticing that this is the third week you've attended church and I wanted to introduce myself and welcome you to our congregation. I'm Graham Atkins and I'm the vicar here at St. Michael's." He paused while he waited for us to respond, my mouth was so dry I couldn't say anything and just stared back at him idiotically, fortunately Joan responded by introducing us and explaining that we did live locally and we had in fact been married in this church many years ago. She looked over at me lovingly, but I could see concern in her eyes that I was still unable to join in the conversation, so she continued by thanking him for the service, we'd both enjoyed it, and assured the vicar of our intention to attend regularly. I nodded mutely as he thanked and expressed his hope that he would see us again, he then left to speak with other members of his 'flock' who were trying to sneak away. As we watched him go Joan whispered with a snigger in her voice.

"He thinks you're a mute." My moment of paralysis was passed, and we just managed to suppress our laughter until we were safely inside the car.

"Fuck, it's straight home for me for a complete change of underwear," I laughed as I started the car, " I thought we'd been caught when the vicar called to us, what a fright. I just couldn't get my mouth to work, sorry about that."

"I know, I wasn't much better, but I realised I had to say something when I saw your face frozen with your mouth open, you really did look guilty, I can't imagine what he thought about us. I've decided to change your name to Woody the Mute!" We both laughed and as we drove away down the road Joan shouted at the top of her voice.

"Fuck in Hell, we've done it, we've pulled it off, I can't believe we've just robbed £10,000 and no one has been hurt. Let's go straight home and open some champagne while we count our money, we deserve a celebration." She sat looking out the front of the car, almost dancing to some silent tune in her head before she nodded her head and shouted again, "Fuck, fuck, fuck, fuck, and I'm sorry about the language, I just feel ecstatic." We both laughed again at her outburst that expressed both our feelings of relief and joy.

CHAPTER 7.

IT TOOK US DAYS to fully calm ourselves and begin to refocus. £10,000 was a sizeable amount of money and we could afford to sit back for a few months and enjoy our ill-gotten gains. But that wasn't how we felt, we had found a new purpose in our lives and we wanted to make money; we did however promise ourselves a small holiday after our next project. We also wanted to complete a second project as we suspected the first, involving Andrew Johnson, had been a very lucky and straightforward exercise and wanted to see if it could be repeated; we suspected it would require a much greater effort in future.

While we considered what we should do next, Joan had done what she'd suggested and began to go to the hairdressers every week. She listened to the conversations and also expanded her circle by joining the local health club; she started by trying yoga classes but gained nothing from the first couple of sessions, people only wanted to talk about yoga and Joan found the movements demanded by the teacher a bit ambitious for her untrained body. But in the coffee bar afterwards, where everyone from all the activity groups met up, it was a hive of local news and gossip and she quickly started to gain some knowledge of who was doing what to whom and began to prepare a small list of individuals that required further investigation.

I wasn't idle either. I went in search of petnapping opportunities. As I observed various dog owners I realised that many of them, particularly the type I was interested in, watched over their pets as if they were children, babies even as some of them were pushed around in little prams decorated with pretty pictures of 'doggie' unicorns, stars and rainbows. I couldn't believe I hadn't noticed this phenomenon before. I followed several of these much-loved pets in their prams or the arms of their owner or on very rare occasions, walking, secured by brightly colored and bejeweled leads. Never did I ever see these 'cutie' pets tied up outside a shop or left anywhere unsupervised.

After many hours of watching and following, I was beginning to feel a little frustrated. 'Petnapping' had seemed like an obvious and quite straightforward plan, but it was starting to appear impracticable as there was to be little or no opportunity to take one of these prized animals, unlike the numerous 'mutts' that people allowed to stray or were tied up without any concern to a lamp post; no fancy little prams for them!

Finally, one couple I followed led me to a Pet Care Salon just off the high street, a facility I didn't know existed. They lifted their little 'fur baby' out of its pram and carried it into the shop, I followed them in, out of pure curiosity, and was instantly amazed at the the quality of the shop fittings and that the products on sale were obviously of high, luxury quality and both of the shop assistants would not have been out of place in the beauty department of a large store, their uniforms were smart and their smiling faces were enhanced with professional make up and styled hair..

An ornate price list on the wall guided clients to the full range of services that were available – strictly by appointment. These services included a Mud Bath, Washing, Styling, Cut or Handstripping, Nail Trimming and Ear Cleaning. A smile crossed my face as I thought I could benefit from all these things myself, except for the prohibitive cost which was between £25 and £150 for each individual treatment.

The couple and their pet, who was apparently called Daisy, were obviously well known to the two glamorous assistants who fussed over the little dog to the point it must've been bruised by the amount of patting and stroking inflicted on it. One of the assistants finally turned to me and with a smile, that showed a full set of sparkling blue/white teeth asked.

"Good morning sir, can I help you?"

"Yes," I replied, "my daughter has two dogs and is coming up to stay with us. She's very particular about her dog's hygiene, diet and appearance and I said I would come in to see what facilities and products you have available so I can report back."

"I think your daughter will find that we can provide for all her doggie needs. What breed of dogs are they?"

I had been preparing myself for this question and had looked up some valuable dog breeds and pictures online so I wouldn't be kidnapping a worthless mongrel. The breed I particularly remembered was a 'Puggle', which was apparently a cross between a Pug and a Beagle (a non-smoking one I hoped!) and I have to say, an extremely cute little dog. "Puggles, a boy named Chico and a girl named Lola." I informed with a proud, confident air.

"Oh, my goodness," exclaimed the assistant, raising her arms in surprise that created a small crackle of static from her quality blouse that pulled tightly against her figure, "Puggles, they're wonderful. We only have one client who has a Puggle, her name is Lulu and we provide all her feed, supplements, treatments and therapies. How lucky your daughter is to have two of them." I tried not to think of the aggressive half breed my daughter had rescued from the shelter, that had finally, after several months, recovered from Mange; its period of suffering had been made even worse during its recovery as it had struggled to scratch since it lost one of its back legs when the heavy front door of her house had blown shut and crushed it. Fortunately, they had named it 'Jason' rather than 'Lucky,' the name the children had originally wanted to call him because they thought he'd been lucky to be saved by them.

"Let me show you around and then I can give you a list of our products and salon treatments." She led me around the shop, pointing out the huge array of different products: - Dog collars with bows, crystal studs and stars in rainbow colours and in every size. Leads in every colour and fabric that were stretchy, short, long, thin, extendable and all available in colour matching shades. Then there were harnesses in a multitude of styles; one even had a handle on the top for easy recovery. There was a large area of the shop dedicated to 'Doggie Beds'; one of which was styled to form a tree house, another designed as 'bunk beds', which Jade, my 'personal assistant', suggested would be the perfect welcoming gift for my daughter's dogs and at only £145.00 would be something they could snuggle into every night and remember what a kind 'Grand-daddy' they had. I was definitely struggling a little bit at this moment to maintain my composure, fortunately I think Jade must have suspected that the 'Grand-daddy' reference may have been a step too far and quickly shuffled us along to the next display area, 'Dog toys'. I think even Jade was beginning to sense that this was all a bit ridiculous and said nothing except "These are our selection of toys," so we both stood looking in silence at the range of soft cuddly toys, soft chewy toys, soft toys to carry around in your mouth – or the dog's if they wanted. All varieties came in a wide ranging selection of animals, from sheep to mermaids, crocodiles to penguins and were all brightly coloured to ensure that the most depressed of dogs would be cheered to receive any of these wonderful things that offered the recipient hours of fun and enjoyment.

Unfortunately they didn't have that effect on me and my feeling of depression only increased as Jade led us around the corner, and with an enthusiastic look and a wave of her hand, in a 'TahDah!', type of gesture to indicated we had reached the highlight of the tour, the 'Clothing and Costume section. This was outrageous; there were clothes for every occasion, gender and size of dog. There were puffer jackets for those cold days when the dog needed to venture out of the pram, a tweed coat for those hunting, shooting, fishing weekends, hoodies for drug dealings, Christmas jumpers, a kimono outfit with golden bows (Jade's favourite!), a skirt outfit for those summer party evenings and a pink Tutu with ribbons for those special ballet lessons. These were a few of the things that immediately caught my attention or were presented to me by my Personal Assistant.

The shop was getting busier but there was no deterring Jade who was on a mission to ensure that I fully understood what was expected of myself and my family when my daughter arrived by way of treating our 'babies' to a lifestyle that befits Puggles. I was escorted through to the rear 'treatment salon' where two girls where focused on a little white bedraggled creature who was undergoing what appeared to be a shampoo and set. As we entered its eyes caught my own and I'm sure I sensed its thoughts – "Please kill me now", it pleaded. Looking to the side of the room I saw there were two other dogs in separate 'luxury' enclosures and trying to show an interest I asked Jade about them. She seemed thrilled to be able to help and explained that the salon offered a "Treat while you shop" service where they looked after and spoilt your pet with treats and treatments while you went off to shop and have lunch or afternoon tea and drinks.

I couldn't take any more; it had been my intention to follow the original couple back out of the shop and discover more of their habits, but I needed some alone time and walked back to the high street and sat on a bench. I felt very depressed, was this what life had degenerated to. Did we leave children hungry and cold while our dogs were dressed in designer jackets and bow ties, slurping specialty doggie ice cream from a gluten free, vegan cone. I hadn't realised until I began to look for potential petnapping victims that so many people had a 'designer' dog as a pet. As I lifted my eyes, trying to raise my spirits, I suddenly saw the couple from the shop coming towards me pushing their dog pram with Daisy's little face poking out the front, occasionally yapping bravely when another dog passed by using those four strange appendages that stuck out below its body. I decided they must be destined to be followed, so as to appear innocent I pretended to read my senior bus pass until they were well past before casually following them, trying to be as inconspicuous as possible.

I watched their every move, they seemed to be simply walking around aimlessly, stopping every few minutes to allow other dog enthusiast to pet and stroke Daisy and admire all her jewelry and outfits. I did eventually realise that this is what they did, this was their 'hobby', this dog was their everything to them, they were so proud. Slowly they eventually left the High Street and began to walk at a brisker pace down several streets, finally turning into a very pretty, tree lined avenue and going into number 7, a smart three-story brick built Victorian house. I continued to walk past to the end, turning left at an intersection where after about 100 metres I turned left again, up what was obviously a small rear 'service' road, which was lined both sides by mature hedging. Each house had its own rear gate that were conveniently numbered, and I quickly came upon number 7.

I could partially see through the hedge into a well-kept garden with a manicured lawn. I quickly stepped back to the cover of the wooden gate when I heard the back door of the house open and could now only observe through a hole where a knot had fallen out of the wood. I watched as Daisy leapt out of the door, no longer constrained in her pram she seemed full of excitement at her freedom to run around her 'patch' where there was a plethora of toys for her to play with. Unfortunately, she completely ignored her toys and galloped down the garden, barking with her high pitched 'yippy, yappy' bark, straight towards where I was hiding behind the gate. I didn't move, I wanted to see what happened and whether anyone would take any notice. Daisy stood one side of the gate barking non-stop and I stood on the other, watching the back door and the rear windows to see if anybody even looked out. Nobody appeared or seemed to show any interest at all, so I spoke to Daisy in a soothing voice.

"It's alright Daisy, it's only me." Incredibly she instantly stopped and when I crouched down and peered around the gate post, continuing to reassure her with gentle words, she immediately came to the gate post and stood wagging her little tail. I said goodbye and walked away, I'd seen all I needed to see and had hatched a simple plan.

As I retraced my steps back into town, I reviewed the things I'd noted. The most important was that Daisy was very friendly, obedient and obviously very trusting; she was certainly no guard dog. Other important details were that her owners assumed she was completely secure in the back garden and ignored or had become 'deaf' to her barking, I wondered if the neighbours had the same feeling of detachment. Also, there was a wire 'link' fence that ran around the inside face of the hedge that came around and was fastened to the gate post, obviously this fence was to stop Daisy escaping or other animals entering. My final important observation was that the small lane was not well maintained and the hedges on both sides were quite overgrown.

It was time to return home for lunch, I was starving, probably with all the exercise and couldn't walk past Greggs without treating myself to a sausage roll, which I ate before getting in the car as I knew Joan would smell it if we were to go out for a drive later. The thoughts of my guilty, secret pleasures made me smile.

CHAPTER 8.

MOST EVENINGS Joan and I would talk while having drinks and supper, comparing notes of what we'd learnt and how our future opportunities were developing. I told her that I had identified an easy petnapping opportunity and about my visit to the pet shop, the fake Puggle dogs our daughter Liz has, and my observations of Daisy, her 'parents' and her garden. I also told her of my plan, and how we must start preparing an area either in the house or the garage to create temporary housing for out kidnap 'victim'. We decided we couldn't shut a dog like Daisy in the garage and therefore agreed to put her in the kitchen where it was warm, but I would have to go back to the 'posh' pet shop and buy a small dog bed, some toys, bowls and food; I felt sure Jade would be thrilled to see me, although I did think she might wonder why I wasn't buying two of everything for the arrival of my two 'grandchildren', but I'd planned a plausible explanation in case she asked.

We agreed that I would progress with the kidnapping of Daisy alone as I felt I could manage this by myself. Joan however, did seem a little disappointed that we weren't doing it together, but other than her acting as the getaway driver I couldn't think of a role for her, and there was no point in both of us being exposed to any risk.

Joan had also been busy. One of her new 'friends' in the hair salon had been telling her about how she now did all her shopping online, she'd decided some months ago that she was fed up with the selection and cost of almost everything on the High Street and had begun initially by buying a new electric kettle from Amazon, which incredibly was delivered the very next day. From that moment on her online purchases had grown to include just about everything, except fresh bread, underwear, and having her hair cut and styled in the salon. She had all her groceries delivered; the delivery man even lifted them into the kitchen. She now spent hours in the comfort of her own home choosing clothes, make-up, shoes and all her household goods; all delivered free to her door. The hair stylist tried to maintain an interest, but as the women droned on and on, she appeared to go into 'auto-pilot', smiling and nodding and making encouraging noises at appropriate times. The woman hair styling finished she went to the counter to pay. Joan had listened intently, she intended to follow this woman and find out where she lived, but as luck would have it the stylist asked if she would like to receive information about their special events and the product range the shop offered; the stylist made the woman laugh as she advised that the salon also offered home visits and their products could be ordered on line for home delivery. The client agreed and immediately gave her name, quite loudly, as Mrs. Barbara Stoddard and her home address and telephone number, which Joan memorized.

Barbara had obviously driven into town as her house was a few miles away, so Joan had had to wait for me to return with the car from Daisy's house before we went off together after lunch to investigate.

The Stoddard's residence was a detached brick-built house, set back a little from road on a pretty avenue of similar houses. We stopped the car just before the entrance drive that went slightly uphill to a single garage attached to the house, from this position we could easily keep watch.

"Do you think one of us should go knock on the door," asked Joan.

"Well that would have to be me," I replied, "as I think she may recognize you from the hairdressers."

"Please," interrupted Joan, "it's a Hair Salon, only poor people go to a 'hairdresser', and the people that work in a Hair Salon are called Technicians, not hairdressers. If we're going to rob these people you really must understand the quality of person you're dealing with." We both laughed.

"Well, I think the Hair Technician made a great job of your hair, you look lovely," I put my hand up to stop her interrupting, "and before you try to distract me further from our mission, I think we ought to sit quietly and watch, there are really only two things we want to learn: The first is how deliveries are made, I can see the front door but there's also a side door they may go to. And the other thing is, do they have a dog?"

"A small dog wouldn't be a problem, but a large one could cause us real problems, I don't fancy arguing with a defensive Alsatian." Joan stated.

"Unless you shot it with your toy gun….." I was interrupted by Barbara coming out of the side door, walking to the car, removing a small box and returning to the house, she was followed by two cats that ran in amongst her legs, it was incredible that she didn't trip over them.

"Well, I think that answers the dog question," Joan commented, "Barbara is obviously a cat person."

We continued to sit quietly in the car, watching the street and particularly Barbara's house. It was surprisingly quiet, only a mother and a small child in a pushchair walked past and no more than half a dozen cars passed in the hour we waited. There was no movement in or around the house until a van pulled up in front of the entrance, the driver got out, opened the rear doors and removed two parcels and walked up the drive to the front door and rang the bell. Nobody answered so he rang the bell again, this time Barbara appeared holding her gardening gloves in her hand. She directed the delivery man to put the parcels just inside and then signed his device before shutting the door. The delivery driver strode back down the drive and drove away.

"I think that was another Amazon delivery and we now know which door she would normally expect to receive parcels. Perfect. Let's go home, we've seen what we wanted, and I think Barbara is an ideal victim."

"The only other concern I have with your plan is that I need to hold the husband hostage while you go off with Barbara, in this instance, to get some money. What happens if she hasn't got a husband, how do we ensure she does what we want her to do?" I asked.

"No husband would be a bonus, you just threaten to kill her cats instead," suggested Joan with an evil smile on her face.

"Of course, I never thought of that, good idea." Joan never ceased to amaze. "Can I suggest that instead of going straight home we go into town and begin to organise the 'props' we'll need, if I remember they are an empty box, two toy guns, two balaclavas, two pairs of gloves and two sacks to go over our victims head."

"Well, it may surprise you to learn that over the past couple of weeks, while you've been chatting up shop assistants and trailing around the countryside, I've been knitting and sewing and have everything ready, except the toy guns and the empty box, which you can get when you go into town tomorrow to get the pet supplies ready for when you kidnap Daisy."

"Wow, well done, can we have a 'fashion parade' tonight, I can't wait to see us in our balaclavas, what colour are they?" I asked.

"They're black, and I've already tried mine on and I've chosen a complete outfit to go with it; black shoes, black trousers and a black roll neck jumper, so yes, we can have a 'fashion parade' tonight but you need to get some black clothes as well so we both look like professional thieves." She laughed at me as I pulled a face.

"Right, 'fashion parade' tomorrow night after I've been shopping in the morning, I need to make a list so I don't forget anything, are you sure you don't want to come with me and help?"

"No, I can't," replied Joan, "I'm going to a flower arranging class with Mary from next door, it's being held at the church hall, it's the first one and she doesn't want to go by herself."

"OK," I replied grumpily, "I'll manage by myself; you just go off and have a good time."

"I will," replied Joan, "you never know what else I might learn, apart from flower arranging, and who else I may meet."

"Our 'business' opportunities certainly seem to be expanding, and with what we're planning to do next it does make me a little nervous. I do know however, that I'm really enjoying all these new plans and experiences and I can see that you are as well. We both seem to have lost a little weight and seem fitter with our more active lifestyle, what do you think?" I asked Joan.

"I agree, I'm really enjoying all the planning and preparation, but like you, particularly now we're about to carry out another two 'missions' almost at the same time, I do feel nervous, even just talking about it, more so than when we blackmailed Andrew Johnson, which somehow was less 'personal'.

"Yes, that's exactly it, blackmailing Andrew never involved us meeting him 'physically' and is therefore so different to actually stealing someone's pet or worse still holding a person to ransom while getting their partner to get some money. It does sound appalling what we're planning to do, but it's all for a good cause, us!"

"I think we should skip a cup of tea when we get home and open a bottle of wine to celebrate our evil plans and the fun we'll have carrying them out," suggested Joan, an idea I couldn't disagree with, I couldn't think why Joan was thinking of drinking tea when we got back anyway.

CHAPTER 9.

JOAN LEFT JUST AFTER 9.30 am and I left 5 minutes later to drive into town. I'd decided that I would shop for my 'criminal' clothes to match the ones Joan had bought for herself: - black boot style trainers, black socks, black trousers with matching belt, black shirt with a black tee shirt to go on underneath and a black jacket, I even bought myself a pack of two, black boxer shorts and wondered if Joan had also bought some black underwear, nothing would surprise me about Joan at the moment. This clothes shopping took most of the morning and by the time I'd had a coffee it was approaching midday when I got to the pet store, which I hadn't realised on my previous visit was called PAWS IN PARADISE. As I entered, I could see it was again remarkably busy, but it gave me time to have another look around before Jade came over while I was looking at the pet beds.

"Welcome back, have you decided to treat your daughter's two Puggles to a new bed for when they come to stay?" I looked back at Jade with a sad face, I think I even managed to squeeze a tear into one corner and with a shaky voice I replied.

"Oh Jade, there's been a terrible accident."

"Oh my god, what's happened?" she asked sympathetically, putting a comforting hand on my arm, "Is it the twins?" It took me a moment to understand that she was referring to my daughter's two fictitious dogs.

"Yes, I'm afraid it is, Chico is dead." I said, really milking the moment with hand over my eyes, shaky voice drama.

"Oh my god," she exclaimed for a second time, "no, no, no, you poor man, that's the worst possible news," her hands covered her face and I could see tears in her eyes. "Please come through and sit down so we can share your family's grief." Hell, I thought I could 'milk' the moment, but her reaction couldn't have been more dramatic if I'd told her that my 'real' grandchild had died. I'd only started this charade as a means of explaining why I was only buying one of everything rather than two, and the 'special' bunk beds couldn't be an option.

She led me by the arm, everybody in the shop stood watching with a reverential silence that befitted someone who had lost everything that was important to them in the world. I was really regretting my choice of excuse as the three therapists in the rear shop stopped their treatments to offer up their heartfelt grief for my loss, how did they know of Chico's death, had everyone been listening to Jade and my conversation, were they all psychic? I was desperately trying to think of how I would continue with my fantasy when we arrived in a small, but very well fitted staffroom where we sat down, Jade faced me and asked.

"Tell me what happened and what I can do to help you manage your loss?" She asked like a qualified bereavement counselor.

"I'd rather not, it's too soon to talk about, it only happened yesterday and they still haven't completed the search, so there's always hope, but I know in my heart that Chico has gone, don't you agree?" I asked Jade as I gazed into her eyes with extreme pathos. I could see however that she wasn't or couldn't leave it there, she had to know, you could sense the presence of the entire shop holding their breaths, hoping that Princess Jade would do the right thing and demand an explanation of what had happened to Chico.

"It always helps to talk about these things and release your grief so you're better able to support your family in these trying moments." This girl was a real master at this game and I knew I had no choice but to tell her the truth, but I kept my head in my hands and stretched the moment out for as long as I could before I just blurted out.

"He was snatched out of my daughter's garden by an eagle." There was a huge intact of breath as the shock of the event was finally revealed. "The bird came out of the sky and with a single talon took him as quickly as any hand of God, my daughter said he disappeared before anyone could react, there was nothing they could do. Chico has gone." I thought I'd better stop there, but then thought better of it as I sensed an opportunity to gain a discount off my purchases growing. "My daughter and two grandchildren are driving up to stay with us for a few days and I remembered how kind and helpful you'd been, I thought I would come back and ask for your help in providing everything I'll need to make Chico's sister, Lola, feel welcomed in what must be a very traumatic time for her."

"I know exactly what she'll need, please stay quietly there Mr. Woody, I'll bring you a cup of tea and then get everything prepared." What a lovely girl, I thought, her parents must be so proud of her. I sat quietly waiting for her to return and I had just finished my tea and the two chocolate biscuits that had been served alongside, when Jade returned and advised, still in a subdued voice.

"I've selected a pretty pink, soft and snuggly bed, it is a little plain but all the others have stars, clouds, suns and moons on them and I didn't want to remind Lola of anything associated with the sky and it was the same for the water and food bowls. I've also included two matching 'guest' towels, our most popular pink velvet evening dress in a small size with a matching coat, because it can still be cool if she has to get out of the car, a beautiful collar and lead, and a selection of toys that I know she'll just love and will help take her mind of things. For her meals I've chosen some 'princess muesli' for her breakfast and a selection of different gourmet dinners. I cannot think of anything else she'll need other than our thoughts and love."

"Jade, you've been so kind and I cannot thank you enough for all your gentle understanding, I feel so much better and stronger to help with my family's grief and I know Lola will know she's loved when she arrives to see all her new things. Thank you again for all your help, please tell me how much I owe you."

"The total amount comes to £296 48p." I waited for her to say that she had spoken to her manager and agreed to deduct 50% discount or something, but she just stood there with a sweet smile on her face.

"Fucking bitch," I thought as I realised she wasn't the caring sympathetic young woman I thought she was, but just someone who was determined to make a sale at any price. I felt cheated, I felt I deserved some reward for my award-winning performance or as it'd turned out, a non-award-winning performance. I accepted that I'd probably misled myself but decided not to tell Joan what I'd spent on temporary accommodation and food for the imminent arrival of Daisy. A final thought occurred to me as I produced my credit card.

"Do you sell a special, irresistible treat that I can offer to Lola when she arrives that will let her know I'm her friend?"

"I know just the thing," advised Jade as she walked off with my credit card, quickly returning with a small packet of soft, chewy biscuits that she put into one of my carrier bags and passed me the card reader so I could enter my code number, I could see that the price had risen further to £303.98; £7,50 for a little bag of stale biscuits was ridiculous, but I decided to pay up and shut up. I thanked her again for all her 'kindness' but I think she sensed the lack of warmth in my words and was already 'lathering' herself over another client before I'd even got out of the door with all my bags. "Fucking bitch," I recited as I walked down the road back to the car, placing all these 'doggie' treats beside my 'criminal' outfit.

"Bugger and Damn," I swore as I realised I'd forgotten to purchase one of the most important items from the pet shop, a pet carry case that I would need to contain Daisy, but realised I would probably needed a mortgage to have bought one there and decided to visit some charity shops to see if they had one.

By the time I'd found what I wanted, I was starving and called Joan to see if she would enjoy some fish and chips, if I brought some home. Her phone rang and rang before going to voice mail, I hung up and bought two fish suppers anyway and drove home to find that Joan had just arrived, so we immediately sat down to eat.

"How was the flower arranging lesson this morning," I mumbled with a mouthful of delicious fresh cod, crunching on the crispy batter, holding a chip in my fingers ready to push it into my mouth as soon as space became available.

"Not very interesting, I only went along to see if I could 'spot a victim' as you always put it, but they were all really dull and Mary next door has to be the dullest of them all. Her driving is something to behold, she has the seat as far forward as it'll go so she's pressed right up against the steering wheel and looks very uncomfortable, then she seems to bend even further forward so her face is almost touching the windscreen. It must've taken us 20 minutes to drive the couple of miles there, never once did she ever go above 20 mph, the only consolation was that we didn't encounter any traffic as it was all stuck behind us." She paused for breath and another mouthful of food.

"How did you get on?" she asked.

"Great. I've bought all my 'criminal' clothes so we can have a fashion parade after lunch. I also bought everything needed to kidnap Daisy the dog and keep her comfortable and fed while she's staying with us." I was interrupted by the front doorbell ringing, both of us paused eating and looked at each other. We both knew the postman had already been, he'd only brought one letter for Joan advising her that a bowel testing kit would come in the next few days and what she should do with it. Ever since we had blackmailed Andrew Johnson, we always had a moment of concern whenever the doorbell rang. I wiped my hands and stood up.

"I'll see who it is," and walked out into the hall and opened the door. A delivery driver stood there with two small parcels in his hand. He hurriedly thrust a sheet at me to sign; he was obviously in a rush and I'd been too slow in answering the door, so he was grumpy. He pushed the parcels into my arms and with a gruff "goodbye" he rushed back to his van and sped off.

I smiled as I realised what had been delivered, it was the 'chip reader' to scan for the identity and contact details for dogs and more excitingly, the 'voice disguiser'; I couldn't wait to try it out by calling Joan and experimenting with different voice settings. After finishing our lunch, I left Joan in the kitchen and went through to the sitting room to set up. It was extremely easy and within moments I had it turned on and connected to my phone, selecting

'Deep Voice' as my first disguise. I called Joan and when she answered and I spoke I even startled myself as this deep, mechanical voice boomed into the phone, I sounded a bit like Darth Vader on steroids. I could hear Joan laughing down the phone, I decided to experiment and turned the setting to 'Baby Girl' and when I spoke again I couldn't believe how ridiculous I sounded, like I'd inhaled some helium. It obviously entertained Joan as not only could I hear her laughing on the phone, I could also hear her through the walls. I suggested that we change places so Joan could speak through the voice changer and I could see what it sounded like.

I showed her how it worked and how to change the settings and went through to the kitchen.

"Hello?" I asked and the little girl's voice replied.

"Hello, have you seen my mummy?" It sounded so funny I couldn't help but laugh, but finished up bent double, hardly able to breathe as Joan commenced a disgraceful conversation with herself switching between different voices.

"No little girl, not since I took her upstairs and gave her a good 'Rogering'," replied the deep voice.

"Is 'Rogering' a sort of present?" asked the little girl's voice.

"It certainly is a very special present?" replied the deep voice.

"Can you give me a 'Rogering'?" asked Joan in her 'normal voice. It took me a moment to stop laughing before replying.

"I suggest we have a cup of tea first to build our strength up, then we could go upstairs and change into our balaclava's and see what happens." Joan was already walking into the kitchen as I put the kettle on.

"What a fantastic piece of equipment, we can have such a lot of fun with it and it'll definitely work making calls for our Ransom negotiations. After we've had our tea I think we should try our full 'criminal' outfits on, to get us in the right mindset and then we should run through our plans for our latest two projects, it's going to be a busy week and hopefully a very lucrative one."

CHAPTER 10.

WE FINISHED OUR FASHION parade upstairs and were very pleased with everything we'd either bought or Joan had made, there were only a few items that were still needed and I offered to buy them tomorrow from the fancy dress shop next to the toy shop. For all the fun and enjoyment we'd had dressing up and laughing at more idiotic conversations on the voice changer, by the time we returned to the kitchen our moods had become much more serious as we began to discuss our projects and the plans for this week.

"I don't think I'll be able to sleep tonight," admitted Joan, "I'm so anxious about tomorrow night, I know we've talked and planned and rehearsed as best we can how everything will happen, but every moment that passes and we get closer to the time for action, I just wonder if we can succeed; will our legs not just turn to jelly, will we be able to speak and give orders to our victims or will we just freeze and appear foolish?"

"Joan, relax," I tried to sound calm and confident, although my true feelings were similar to hers, "we've practiced everything thoroughly and know exactly what we're doing, I'm not going to let myself 'freeze up' like I did collecting Andrew Johnson's money, that was our first 'mission'; I believe we both faced our demons that day and are much more mentally prepared and stronger for having that experience. What's the worst that can happen?" I asked, answering the question myself quickly before Joan started to prepare a list. "The worst is that everything goes wrong and we turn on our heels and run away. Nobody will follow us as they'll still be uncertain if our guns are real or not, even when they call the police we'll be well gone and as long as we're careful we won't have left any evidence that could identify us. Everything will be fine, just relax." I again repeated.

Neither of us slept well that night and other than my brief trip to the shops the following morning, we couldn't concentrate and settle to do anything constructive in the house for the entire day; we tried to read, we tried to watch some television, we tried to do some jobs about the place, we constantly moved around trying to keep ourselves occupied and it was with some relief when 5.00pm arrived and it was time to get ready. We suddenly had a purpose as we started dressing and preparing for real, there was no more foolishness with the voice changer, we were completely focused as we went through our checklist before getting into the car to drive to Barbara Stoddard's house.

We parked opposite the gate to her house so we could watch who went in and see the front door, even when we sat low in our seats. We saw there were no cars in the drive and after watching for about thirty minutes we didn't see any movement inside the house. It was another thirty minutes before Barbara drove past us and turned into her drive, parked, took several bags out of the car and carried them into the house. We continued watching, pretending to look at a map on the very few occasions anybody walked or drove past, but nobody else went into Barbara's house.

As darkness settled lights appeared in several windows, including upstairs and we identified which window was Barbara's bedroom as we saw her closing the curtains, the light remained on for several minutes before it went off. We then saw her at the kitchen window. Joan was looking through the binoculars and commented.

"She's obviously not going out because she's got her dressing gown on, I don't think we should leave it much longer, she may be having an early night." I could hear the shakiness in her voice, and in my own as I agreed.

"OK then, let's go." We both got out of the car, put our 'guns' in our jacket pockets, put on our wooly gloves, took the cardboard box containing the pet carry case out of the boot and briskly walked towards the house, pulling on our balaclava's as we moved. We made a splendid sight as I caught sight of our reflection in the glass of the front door as we approached. Our matching outfits of black everything, including our balaclava's, highlighted the only non-black areas of our eye, nose and mouth holes; it made us look very sinister and intimidating; a little too much like terrorists, which was a bit unfortunate but decided it may help ensure that our 'victims' did as we told them.

We put the cardboard box on the front doorstep, took out our guns, stood to the side of the door and rang the bell. I looked across at Joan and saw the concentration in her eyes, she seemed so determined and when Barbara opened the door and reached down to pick up the box, it was Joan who sprang forward like some American cop holding her gun with both hands and instructed Barbara with such force to 'BACK UP' that the woman almost fell back into the house. I picked up the box and followed them in, closing the door behind.

"Sit down," instructed Joan, still with her forceful, authoritative voice. When Barbara was seated on a hall chair, I tied each of her hands to the frame and Joan held up our typed questions and instructions, which we'd carefully typed on cards. The first card read: -

"Please answer ALL questions truthfully and carry out ALL instructions without variation and nobody or no animals will be harmed. Do you understand?"

"Yes," said Barbara nodding her head. Joan put up another question card asking:-

"Are you in the house by yourself?"

"Yes," she again replied.

"Are you expecting any visitors tonight?" Was the next question card.

"No," she answered shaking her head.

Joan held up another card.

"We want your money. We don't want anything else. Do you have any money in the house and where is it?"

"There is some money in my safe and a little bit more in my handbag," Barbara replied shakily.

Joan now held up her final card which detailed exactly what was going to happen. This card read:-

"We are going to untie you so you can retrieve this money. You are then going to collect ALL your credit and debit cards and I will then direct you to drive me to a cash point where you will withdraw £400 from each account. You will then return to the car and drive back here to the house. Do you understand?"

While Barbara was reading these cards and answering Joan's questions, I walked around the house searching for the cat, or cats as I observed two empty food bowls in the huge utility room. One of the cats was asleep in a luxurious bed and without any difficulty or initial objection, I lifted it into the carry case, which I had previously lined with a soft blanket where it settled back to continue its sleeping. I had to pause to admire the volume and quality of equipment that was housed in this room, a room that was bigger than our entire kitchen at home. The washing machines; one huge, fully automatic, in stainless steel with a multitude of complex looking programes, sat beside a smaller washing machine, equally smart but with fewer complexities and was obviously for washing the cats 'laundry' as it had a picture of a cat stuck to it with the names Sofie and Jason. There was then a large tumble dryer and a dishwasher, both in stainless steel, a tall, double door 'American' style fridge and an equally huge freezer unit. At one corner there was an array of outdoor boots and shoes all racked in dryer units and to the side of this was a large drying cupboard that housed all types of outdoor clothing. On top of the worktops proudly stood a huge variety of matching equipment; food mixers, coffee maker, kettle, toaster, the list could go on. Incredibly, the kitchen itself was three or four times as large and much of the equipment that was present in the utility room was duplicated here, but supported by a black four oven Aga, a black gas stove and racks of pans. The room was completed by a centrally placed, twelve-seater, light oak dining table and chairs, all made up with sparkling place settings, water and wine glasses, napkins etc. All ready for a 'light' supper.

My overall impression was that hardly anything in either the kitchen or the utility room was ever used, it spent its life 'posing' to impress any visiting guests or in our case, thieves!

I walked back into the hall with the cat contained in the carry case and saw Barbara's look of concern as she saw one of her 'babies' incarcerated.

"Please don't hurt Sofie, I've already promised to do as you've asked," she pleaded. Joan went behind her to remove the restraints so Barbara could lead them to her safe, which turned out to be behind a false panel in the cloakroom. After it was opened I stepped forward to examine the contents; there were many 'legal' looking documents and three jewelry boxes that I carefully opened with some difficulty with my thick woolen gloves, all three were full of rings, necklaces and bracelets, all very tempting but I put them back where I'd found them. The item that particularly interested me was an old-fashioned tin money box, the type secretaries used to keep the petty cash in, which may have reflected Barbara's original career as the box contained her petty cash, a sizeable amount by the selection of £50, £20 and £10 notes that were neatly clipped together. I put the cash in my jacket pocket, shut the safe and picked up the case where Sofie continued to sleep. I waited in the sitting room while Joan took Barbara upstairs to get dressed, returning just to indicate they were leaving to visit, for the first time, the cash point machine.

I checked my watch, It was now 9.35pm and when Joan and I rehearsed this journey it took approximately 15 minutes to drive there, we then allowed a further 15 minutes for removal of cash, this was dependent on the number of cards Barbara had, and from the appearance of her purse she had several so it may take a little longer, nevertheless I expected them to return by no later than 10.30pm. With almost an hour to 'kill' I decided to have a good look around the house, which although incredibly well fitted and furnished it had the same 'sterile', ornamental, unused feel about everything; it was if it had been staged ready for a photo shoot for Homes and Garden magazine. I couldn't find anything on display, other than a few family pictures and one or two well read books to indicate that anybody even lived in the house.

I returned to the sitting room and sat quietly wondering what sort of a person Barbara Stoddard was. Was there a Mr. Stoddart? Were there any 'little' Stoddert's? Had something happened to them or were there just never any? Was she just a single woman who'd had a successful career or inherited a fortune?

I was disturbed by the cat, Sofie', mewling in the case and was surprised when literally seconds later, as if the animal had a sixth sense, I heard the car pull into the driveway. I checked through the hall window that it was them returning and not a police car and was reassured when I saw Joan's familiar outline following Barbara towards the front door, which I opened in anticipation. I saw the satisfied look in Joan's eyes and the nod of her head that all had gone well. We all returned to the sitting room where Joan tied Barbara to a chair again and we sat in complete silence for ninety minutes before the whole exercise was repeated.

On their second return and again being reassured by Joan's satisfied look and the confident nod of her head, I returned to the hallway, released the cat, who ran straight to Barbara and took shelter between her feet, collected the empty box and we left after Joan had tied only one of Barbara hands to a chair in such a way that she would be able to untie herself, but would take her some time using only one hand.

It felt great to be back in the car driving towards town, and it was a huge relief for us both to remove our balaclavas and wooly gloves. It was even better that we could start talking to each other and I quickly asked.

"How did you get on?"

"It went like clockwork, she was so worried that you'd harm her cats that she'd have done anything, because I never once spoke to her most of the time we just drove in silence. Those instruction notes we prepared worked perfectly. I cannot think of anything we need to change or prepare differently for our next 'mission,' obviously things would be completely different if she'd had a husband. How about you." She asked.

"Well I obviously had the easy task, basically 'cat sitting', there's really nothing to tell. I had a good look around the house, which is absolutely stunning except it's almost like nobody actually lives there; there's nothing personal about it, certainly no sign of a Mr. Stoddart or any children or grandchildren. It seems like Barbara just likes living in a film set mansion all by herself."

"Apart from the cats," Joan added.

"Did you see the jewelry she had in the safe? If we'd been proper 'burglars' there was enough value there to last us and see our pension years out; there was a fortune worth."

"I did see it when you lifted it out and it was very tempting to take, but we did discuss this and if we let our greed take over, that's when we're liable to be caught. We wouldn't know what to do with any of that type of stuff."

"You're right, but it was tempting, and I did think we were missing out on an opportunity at the time, now away from any temptation I know we were right to leave it. How much cash do you think we got altogether?" I asked.

"Quite a lot I think, Barbara had so many credit and debit cards and she spent ages at the cash point and handed me a sizeable wodge when she got back in the car after both visits. When we get home, we can sit and count it, I love that part." Exclaimed Joan.

"Are you hungry." I asked.

"Not really, a bit peckish, I know it's late but a glass of wine and the egg sandwiches we prepared before we left will be just enough for me. I think after that I fancy sitting watching a film or something on the TV, I'm certain I couldn't go to bed and sleep." We sat in silence for a while as we drove home, finally pulling into our drive and parking behind our son's car.

"What the fuck is Mark doing here, we weren't expecting him, were we?" I asked.

"No, I spoke to him last week and he said everything was fine, something must be wrong though, he's driven a long way without telling us he was coming. We'd better leave our balaclavas and the money hidden in the car. Where will we tell him we've been?"

"I can't think. Let's just tell him we decided to have a run out in the car, and we went down to the coast and had some fish and chips."

"Brian, it's 1.30 in the morning, he's not going to believe that and I know we can hardly tell him we've been out robbing a woman in her home but... oh shit, he's coming out to see why were just sitting in the car." We both got out and walked towards him.

"Mark, what are you doing here, have you been here long, we went out for a drive." Joan blurted out. "Come on in." We walked into the kitchen and the first thing I noticed was the sizeable plate of egg sandwiches, our supper, had been reduced to a few crumbs and a screwed-up piece of clingfilm, so I immediately knew he'd been here for some time.

"Sit down and tell us what's happened, and I'll put the kettle on. Have you had enough to eat?" asked Joan glancing down at the empty plate. Mark didn't reply immediately; he was very distracted and fortunately didn't notice or comment on our all black costumes. He sat rubbing his face in his hands before he finally announced.

"Jennifer's having an affair with Jason and I caught them in bed together." He explained in an angry voice. "The school called me at work to say that Heather had been sick and needed collecting from school, they said they'd tried to call her mother but couldn't get through to her, so I went and collected her and took her home. When we got there, I saw Jason's car in our drive, which I thought was odd because he told me on Sunday when we were working out at the gym, that he was away all this week.

Heather and I went into the house and I helped her upstairs as she just wanted to lie down in her bed, I then went into our bedroom and saw them. Jennifer leapt out of bed wrapping a blanket around herself and demanding to know what I was doing home. I just told her that the school had called to say Heather wasn't well, so I picked her up and brought her home. I shut the bedroom door and left; I think I would've killed them both if I'd stayed. I couldn't think of anywhere else to go so I came here."

"Mark, that's a terrible thing to happen, no wonder you're upset. Who is Jason, do we know him?" Asked Joan as she put her arm around him. I took over the tea making duties as the kettle started to boil.

"Jennifer's known him for years, he married Sarah, her best friend from university and was godmother to their son last year. I know him from social gatherings and we both go to the same gym. I thought he was a friend." We sat drinking our tea. Joan and I both hated these types of dramas, it's always a struggle to think of what you can say or what help you can offer, other than tea and sympathy. We were suddenly distracted with a phone ringing, the sound coming from Mark's jacket pocket, he took it out and looked at the screen before pressing the red button to disconnect the call.

"Was that Jennifer?" I asked.

"Yes," was his curt reply, "she's been calling all night, but I won't answer her calls, what can we possibly have to say to each other. Ten years we've been married, how many times has she gone with other men? I thought we were 'soul mates'; how stupid am I." He almost spat the last words he was so angry. We sat in silence again. We'd all finished our tea and I wondered if I should make some more.

"Mark, would you like something more to eat? How about some bacon sandwiches? I'm going to put the kettle on again anyway."

"Not for me Dad, I couldn't eat anything." I could see Joan nodding her head, so I began cooking bacon, the smell was heavenly and had my mouth watering. I spread a dozen slices of bread with butter, I knew what would happen, so I prepared plenty. Setting the table with plates, napkins, tomato and brown sauce, I then put the large plate of sandwiches on the table and watched as Mark dived in, spreading a thick layer of tomato sauce over the bread before his mouth was filled and his jaws went to work. Joan and I both quickly followed his example; it had been a long night for us and I couldn't see it ending anytime soon.

Mark was finishing his third sandwich when his phone rang again.

"You cannot just keep ignoring her Mark, sooner or later you're going to have to speak, even if you finish up shouting at each other, you must sort things out for the sake of the children as well as yourselves." Suggested Joan in a calm voice. Mark looked at her for a moment before pushing his chair back and walking out into the hall, closing the door behind him, which was quite pointless since we could still hear him as he began shouting words and phrases like; 'Slut', 'Fucking Bastard', 'Cheating Whore' that in all probability could be heard throughout the entire neighborhood. Gradually the tirade slowly quietened and after several more minutes of 'normal' conversation, Mark returned, sat back at the table and picked up the last remaining bacon sandwich.

"You were right Mum, Jennifer and I do need to talk, we must sort this out for the sake of the kids, but I don't know how, I don't think I can ever forgive her or trust her again."

"It'll take time and the most difficult part for you will be to forgive her mistake, but you need to ask yourself Mark, why was she tempted by Jason, were you failing her in some way, had you forgotten she was a women, not just your wife and the mother of your children?" Joan's incredibly wise words surprised me never mind Mark, and we both sat silently staring at her for a minute before she continued. "So what do you want to do now, you know you're welcome to stay here if you want, or are you going to go home and begin to resolve the difficulties in your relationship. We are both here to support both you and Jennifer. I will be calling Jennifer, whatever your decision, to tell her that she is still part of our family and we are here if she needs us." Joan stared at Mark as if she dared him to challenge her, she knew him too well, she knew he had many failings himself, and he feared her current neutral stance may turn against him if he did argue. I sat there just wanting everything to go back to normal, I hated any form of conflict or upset and was pleased Joan had taken control.

Again, we sat silently, I even wondered if I should make some more tea as the minutes passed, finally Mark stood up and announced.

"You're right Mum, I can't stay here, I need to go home and sort things out, so when you call her tell her I'm on my way back. He gave his mother a hug and whispered, "Thanks, I'll call you tomorrow." He then thanked me for the tea and sandwiches, put his coat on and moved towards the front door, I picked up our keys and walked out with him as I needed to move our car so he could get out.

After he'd left, I came back into the house with all our stuff, including the carrier bag with all the money. I could hear Joan speaking with Jennifer who seemed to be doing most of the talking. I went into the kitchen, put everything on the table, took two glasses and a bottle of red wine from the cupboard and began to fill both glasses when Joan returned from her conversation.

"I don't think I could take any more drama tonight; my nerves are absolutely shattered." She said, sitting down and swallowing two mouthfuls of wine before continuing. "What a performance, Jennifer has always been a bit of a tart and was quite capable of having a fling with some handsome stud, but I thought she'd be more discreet, stupid girl for taking this Jason guy to her own bed in the family house. But I don't think Mark has been entirely the innocent victim, listening to Jennifer I don't think he's been the most faithful or attentive partner. It's their lives, but I don't want them screwing up our two gorgeous grandchildren."

"I think you handled the situation perfectly; I couldn't have done what you did. Anyway, enough, we've had a very productive 'business' night and I can't wait to count our ill-gotten gains. Do you want to count it?" I asked.

"No, I'm just going to sit and enjoy this wine, I'll watch you, there looks like a hell of a lot."

I began to count. The first bundle was the money from the 'petty cash' tin, there was an unbelievable £1750.

"Why would she keep that amount of money in the house?" I asked, "particularly when she's carrying around another..." I paused as I counted a second smaller bundle of notes, "£340 in her purse?" Joan just kept watching and drinking her wine, not having any answer and probably wishing she could be that extravagant with her cash. The next bundle was from Joan's first trip to the cash point with Barbara and this amount was £1600, the same amount as the final bundle from their second trip. I quickly added the four amounts together and arrived at a total of £5290.

"My God," exclaimed Joan, putting down her wine glass in surprise, "that's a lot of money and a lot more than we ever thought we'd get, I think we just hit lucky with Barbara. I even think she didn't particularly care about the money, she was only really concerned about her cats, and I sensed also her jewelry, the fact that neither of these things were taken or harmed makes me think she won't bother even reporting the crime. What do you think?"

"I hope you're right and we never get to find out with an unwelcome visit! It is a lot of money and makes out total more than £15000 from our first two 'projects', which is a hell of a lot more than I ever thought possible. The next, the petnapping of Daisy; I know I said I would do this tomorrow, but it's been a very long night and I think we deserve a day off, so I'm leaving it until Friday. I've also had a rethink and would like to have your help, if you wouldn't mind, we seem to carry a lot of luck when we're together and it would be simpler if there are two of us. A thought's just occurred to me, it's just as well Mark didn't go into the utility room where all Daisy's bed and stuff are on the floor, he obviously just came in and sat and ate everything out of our fridge!"

"It has been a successful, but an awfully long day and I am definitely ready for bed. I love the idea of having a day off tomorrow, let's decide what we want to do in the morning. Will you hide this money with the rest, perhaps we ought to get a safe installed, it would be terrible if we got burgled, and I'm certain they'd find it easy enough hidden where it is at the back of the cupboard." Joan went upstairs to bed, and while I was clearing everything away I began to worry about being robbed of our newfound wealth; a worry I never had when we had nothing.

CHAPTER 11.

I KNEW THAT DAISY'S 'parents' had been in town last Friday at about 10.00am when I'd followed them to the pet shop, they had then returned to their house at just after 11.30am. Joan and I parked just down from their house at 9.30am and watched for their departure. Joan was in her 'normal' clothes, there wasn't any point for her to be in any form of disguise, I on the other hand, wore working boots, a pair of old cord trousers, a checked shirt, a brown jacket and a flat cap, all of which I'd managed to buy from the charity shop for less than £20.00. To complete the disguise, I wore a pair of glasses I'd had since before I started using contact lenses, and a large, grey moustache; I looked like gentrified landscape gardener and for some reason I started speaking in a west country accent.

"You sound like a pirate; I cannot take you seriously looking and sounding as you do," said Joan as we sat in the car watching for Daisy's departure in her pram. We had been talking about our day out yesterday; we'd set off for a drive down to the seaside but had discovered a quaint country pub and stopped for a drink. When we looked at the menu we couldn't resist and had gorged ourselves on the three-course lunch menu. We'd both chosen the homemade leek and potato soup, Joan then had a huge plate of mince and dumplings while I chose the steak and kidney pie. We should've stopped eating at that point, but the deserts were too difficult to resist, so we both fought our way through a large bowl of sticky toffee pudding, helped down with a jug of custard. We decided to abandon any thought of continuing to the seaside for a walk and instead drove straight home and went to bed for an extended afternoon 'snooze'. A perfect day!

"I think it's because I feel dressed like a country farmer and whenever we talk about the seaside I always think of the west country. Speaking like a swash buckling pirate is not a bad disguise though, maybe for my next petnapping mission I should wear an eye patch as well." We both laughed.

"Here they come." I pointed out, as the couple came out of their front door pushing the pram, I could see Daisy's cute little face peering from underneath the hood, which was drawn up so the breeze wouldn't ruffle her well-groomed appearance. We watched as they walked up the road and disappeared when they turned right towards the high street. I gave them a further 5 minutes before Joan drove the car around the corner and parked at the entrance to the small rear lane. In full disguise and with a hobbling gate to give the impression of a man with an old injury (or perhaps I was trying to impersonate a pirate!), I walked up the lane with my secateurs, in case I needed to pretend to be cutting the hedge if anyone approached, and my pliers to cut loose the corner of the fence where it joined the gate post of Daisy's garden. As no one was about and I was certain I couldn't be seen, it took only a few minutes to loosen the corner of the fence, which I then bent back into position so it still appeared to be intact.

I returned to the car and we drove away and parked several streets away where we waited. At 11.15 we drove back to Daisy's road and again parked where we could watch for their return. We didn't have to wait long before we saw the two proud 'parents' walking down the street pushing their pram; this time they were held up for a few moments as they stopped to talk to an elderly couple who were leading a rather unattractive, almost bald little dog that looked very odd. Daisy was eventually pushed into her house and the front door closed.

Again Joan drove around, parking at the entrance to the little rear lane, where I removed from the boot the pet carry case and the little packet of special treats and set off up the lane until I reached the back gate of Number 7. I peered cautiously through the hedge, there was no sign of Daisy, so I concealed the carrycase in the overhanging branches opposite and began to prune the shrubs while constantly watching for any prying eyes or someone walking down the lane.

After about 10 minutes of this charade, and with a sizeable pile of branch clippings beginning to accumulate, I heard the familiar high pitched 'yippy yapping' that signaled Daisy had been released into the garden and within seconds she was at the gate, peering and barking at me through the exposed bit of fence at the side of the gate post.

"Hello Daisy," I cooed, still sounding a little bit like a pirate, "There, there girl, it's only me." She fell silent, her curiosity and the recognition of familiar words spoken with a calming tone, had her stumpy little tail wagging. "Look what I've got for you." I held out one of the treats through the fence, Daisy sniffed first, took it in her mouth and then stood chewing it, looking at me with almost a smile on her face. I offered her another treat, this time she took it straightaway and again stood contentedly chewing as I pulled the partly cut fence towards me to allow a clear opening for her to come through and take the next treat. Without rushing her I positioned the opened carry case close in front of her and put two pieces of the brown treat towards the back. When Daisy had finished her second morsel she happily walked into the carry case to continue eating the next two.

I gently shut the door engaging the clip to prevent it from opening, pulled the fence back into place, picked up the carry case and walked back to the car, putting Daisy on the back seat and partially covering the case with a pink blanket. I passed another couple of treats in to keep her content and got into the passenger seat before Joan drove us away.

"How did it go? you've obviously got the dog," asked Joan glancing across at me as I removed my disguises. I saw in the little vanity mirror that the moustache had left a reddish mark.

"It was easy, once they let her out into the garden, a few of those treats, which she seemed to find irresistible and she just walked into the carry case." I turned around to look through the gaps to see what the dog was doing and was pleased to see she had lain down and seemed content to watch us around the corner of the pink cover. "She's really quite settled and certainly doesn't seem to be stressed in anyway."

As soon as we arrived home Joan opened the front door and I carried the case straight through to the utility room, Joan followed in behind, shutting the door so Daisy couldn't escape to anywhere else in the house as I opened the case to allow her to come out. Surprisingly, she wasn't in a rush and I had to coax her out with another treat. I splashed the water in the water bowl to show her where she could get a drink and put a few more treats in the other bowl to show where her food was. She sniffed around, accepting both Joan and I's comforting words and stroking.

"When she's settled a bit more, I'll put her lead on and take her out into the garden." Offered Joan who was obviously quite taken with the friendliness of the little animal.

"If you keep her occupied, I'll scan to see if we can gain all her details." I reached over, picking up the scanner and guided it over daisy's neck and shoulders; almost instantly the scanner gave a 'bleep' and a number showed on the screen. I reset and tried again, and the same number appeared.

"It only gives me a number." I told Joan, "I wonder what that means, I thought it would give me the owners contact details."

"When you read up on how these things work, what did it say?"

"Just that the scanner enabled identification of the dog by reading the chip."

"I think you'd better find out what that number means and how you identify the owners with it. In the meantime, there is another more 'old fashioned' way of getting the owners details."

"How's that?" I asked.

"You just read the note that's attached to her collar in the little silver tube." She explained, holding the note up smugly. I was beginning to wonder if my hasty investment in technology had been wasted.

"It has the owner's name and telephone number, which is all we need."

"That's perfect, I'll call them later and tell them we've kidnapped Daisy and we want £2000 to give her back."

"I thought we were only going to ask for £1000?" Joan asked, her forehead creased to emphasise her question, she didn't like having the plans and agreements we'd reached changed on a whim.

"Yes, but I just think with the level of investment we've made the price must go up." I knew as soon as I said this, and Joan looked up at me I'd made a mistake.

"What 'level of investment', we've only bought this obviously useless scanner, which you can probably return, a voice disguiser and a few little things for the dog." She paused, "How much were the dog's things?"

"It wasn't just the money we've invested, but our time as well." I explained calmly.

"How much were the dog's things?" Demanded Joan sensing blood.

"It was important that we provided Daisy and future animals the level of quality they're used to so they feel welcome while staying with us." I moved my foot as I said this so I could stand on the dog's tail to make it jump and act as a distraction; now both Joan and Daisy stared accusingly at me.

"Brian, how much were the dog's things?"

"£303.98 and then another £25.00 for the carry case and £28.00 for the hat, moustache and glasses."

"And £65.75 for the voice changer and £159,99 for the scanner, that's about £580 Brian, that's ridiculous, what the hell cost £303.98 at the pet shop?"

"Joan, these are all quality investments towards our long-term income, this is all just one-off expenditure and I believed it would pay to buy the best to start with." I explained, with my most sincere of expressions and spoken with a caring and persuasive voice.

"Brian, how did you manage to spend £303.98 in the pet shop?"

I wanted to say 'Because I was outmaneuvered by a hard-nosed sales bitch who had great breasts and fluttered her eyelids at me in a persuasive and provocative way,' but instead I simply explained that I didn't think it was too expensive and I would show her the receipt later so she could see how much things had cost.

Daisy and Joan continued to stare at me, obviously not convinced but unable to argue further. I smiled back at their glowers.

"She's a lovely little dog though, isn't she?" Daisy wagged her tail as I stroked her and even Joan smiled and joined in.

"She is a bit cute; I've always wanted a little dog like this ever since I was a child." Joan confessed, my mother had an allergy and dogs particularly made her sneeze; she got a rash if she touched an animal."

"I didn't know that." I said, thinking how I would've bought a dog for Joan years ago if I'd known it would've kept her mother away. She sat quietly continuing to stroke the dog who responded by lying half in her lap.

"I think I'll go and prepare some words to say to Daisy's parents." I picked up the little note and read, 'Sheila and Douglas Evans - Tele: 0712138275'. I got up, walked through to the office, and sat in front of the computer to draft out the words I intended to use when I called them.

Is that (Sheila or Douglas) Evans,

You must be very worried about little Daisy, but have no fear, she is safe and being well cared for, although she does seem a little concerned with the proximity of our two Dobermans Pinschers, they seem to think she is some sort of rabbit and are quite excited at the thought of playing with her out in the fields. These pets do love to play.

We're anxious to get Daisy returned to you and this can be quite straightforward if you agree to pay us £2000 in cash, then she will be returned safely. Do you accept this simple arrangement?

PAUSE FOR ANSWER – YES...?

Please give me your email address.

PAUSE – WRITE DOWN EMAIL ADDRESS.

We will send you instructions by email of how to make the payment and how Daisy will be returned to you. To prove that Daisy is alive and well at this moment, we will attach a photograph with her standing on today's newspaper.

We must instruct you NOT to contact any other person or organisation, including the police. We will be watching and monitoring carefully your actions and if at any time we believe you have not fully followed these instructions you will not hear from us again, nor will you see Daisy again.

Goodbye

I returned to find Joan now in an armchair in the sitting room, Daisy sprawled across her lap.

"Joan, do you think it's a good idea to get too friendly with the dog, I think we should just keep her in the utility room."

"She's fine here, she won't be able to tell anyone what she did or who she was with so we might as well make her stay comfortable, as you keep on emphasizing after your pet shop extravaganza!" I wondered how long Joan would keep up these cutting references, but decided not to say anything, I wanted her comments on what I was going to say to Sheila and Douglas.

"I'm going to call Daisy's 'parents' and this is what I thought I'd say." I passed her the piece of paper, which she quickly read.

"Do you think they'll pay £2000 for Daisy?"

"If she was your dog and you'd 'lost' her, would you pay £2000?" Joan looked at Daisy and thought for a moment.

"You're probably right, but let's wait and see. Apart from the price are you keeping all the other arrangements we agreed the same?"

"Absolutely. Ok, if you're happy I'll go make the call."

"Oh," interrupted Joan, "just one more thing, you're not going to use the little girl voice on the phone, are you?" We both laughed at the thought.

"No, it's got to be the deep, menacing Darth Vader voice. I'm going to shut the doors when I make the call because if you start laughing it'll set me off as well and then they'll never take me seriously." I smiled and walked out and back into the office, closing all the doors behind me.

I sat with the phone in one hand and the voice changer held over the mouthpiece with the other, I paused, trying to settle myself, before pressing the call button on the phone, it only rang twice before it was answered by a breathless, female voice.

"Hello, who's speaking?" she asked. I paused for effect. "Hello," she asked again, this time I replied and was surprised once more how effective the voice changer was, it didn't sound like me at all, it sounded very menacing as I read out my pre-prepared words, pausing only for her to give me the answers and email address I demanded. As I said, "Goodbye," she immediately pleaded for me not to hurt Daisy, she meant everything to her. I hung up thinking we should perhaps have asked for more money.

I turned the computer back on and began to type the agreed email to Sheila and Douglas Evans, this message repeated everything I'd said over the phone, informing them that the 'drop off' would be on Sunday morning at 9.30 am and would give them details on the Saturday night of the exact location and arrangements of where the money was to be left. I also stated that they would receive a call before midday on the Sunday to advise where Daisy could be collected. I read through the email to make sure it was all correct before finally attaching the photograph we'd taken earlier of Daisy and the newspaper. I pressed send.

Within 5 minutes the Evan's sent a reply agreeing to our demands and asking if the payment and return of Daisy could be tomorrow, Saturday instead, they were very anxious to have the safe return of Daisy. I didn't reply but returned to the sitting room to report back to Joan, who was still in the armchair, still with the dog on her lap, but now both were covered with a blanket. After Joan had nodded her head to acknowledge that all was progressing well, she asked if I would turn on the TV and pour some wine, both of which I obliged and left her watching a nature programme that Daisy seemed to enjoy as well. I returned to the computer, I wanted to find out some prices and installation instructions for a safe.

CHAPTER 12.

WE'D GONE TO BED EARLY that night; I was worn out and fell asleep almost straightaway, even though Joan continued to read with the light on. I slept soundly until early on the Saturday morning when I was surprisingly awoken with my face being licked. Initially I couldn't understand why Joan would do this, and I didn't find it particularly pleasant because her breath wasn't all that fresh either. I soon realised that somehow during the night, Daisy had managed to open the utility room, kitchen, and bedroom doors, climb silently onto our bed and stealthily sneaked under the blankets. Or, more realistically I decided, Joan had gone downstairs and brought her up. I was becoming very concerned at the attachment Joan had formed with this little dog, I could understand why, it was very intelligent and very cute, but we should remember it was not ours and it was getting given back the following day.

Having been forced out of bed, I set off down the stairs to the kitchen to make some tea and was followed firstly by Daisy, who stood looking at me with some apparent expectation, and then by Joan who suggested she needed to go outside. I watched as they both went out, Daisy exploring the garden and Joan watching, I took out our cups of tea, passing one to Joan.

"How did the dog get into our bed last night; I was very surprised when I was woken with a raspy tongue licking my face, I thought it was you!"

"I brought her upstairs, she was barking, I'm really surprised you didn't hear her. I couldn't let her make too much noise and disturb the neighbours. She's obviously used to sleeping with her owners and probably felt lonely downstairs." We continued to watch as Daisy trotted around the garden probably wondering why we didn't have any toys for her to play with and after a while she became bored and we all went in.

We got dressed, had our breakfast, did a few chores around the house, generally occupying ourselves knowing that we couldn't leave the house today. It was just past 11.30am when the front door rang, Joan and I looked at each other and quickly put Daisy in the utility room and closed the door, by which time the bell was being rung a second time. When Joan opened it, we were very surprised to see Mark, Jennifer and the two children, Heather and Sean. There was a moment in time when we all just looked at each other, the family waiting to be invited in, Joan and I anxious to conceal Daisy.

"Come in, it's lovely to see you," and as the they all entered there were lots of hugs and kisses as we led them through to the sitting room.

Mark handed Joan some flowers and then Jennifer did the same; she held Joan's hand she said.

"We'd both like to thank you for all your wise words and support the other night, I'm particularly embarrassed by my foolishness. Mark and I have talked about everything and agreed we're going to work hard to make our relationship..." she stopped talking and all eyes, particularly the children's, turned towards the kitchen door where the sound of barking could be heard; I was quite surprised how loud it was given that I knew how small the animal was making the noise.

"Have you got a dog Grandma?" asked Heather excitedly.

"We're looking after a friend's dog for a couple of days," answered Joan casually, "her name is 'Maisie', do you want to come and see her?"

"Yeah!" Both the children shouted and followed Joan into the kitchen and opened the door into the utility room, Daisy, alias 'Maisie' jumped out and ran around the children, jumping up at them as they stroked and played with her.

"She's lovely and she obviously likes children" commented Jennifer.

"Can we have a dog like this?" demanded Sean.

"Yes Mum, can we have a dog like this?" repeated Heather, "me and Sean can look after it."

"I don't think that would be a very good idea," pointed out Mark, "we don't have any garden, our flat is too small and we're all out at school or working during the day; it wouldn't be fair." The children's stopped playing and they both just held 'Maisie' and all three looked up with expressions of disappointment.

"Your Grandad and I have decided to get a little dog like this, haven't we?" Joan looked at me with one of her 'I'll make your life a misery if you say the wrong thing' faces.

"Yes," I replied with a look that told Joan she owed me, "that's why we've bought all this special stuff that 'Maisie's' borrowing during her stay, isn't it darling?"

"It certainly is," agreed Joan with a smile, "and as we haven't found a dog yet would you two children help us choose one?"

"Yeah!" shouted the children, bouncing up and down with 'Maisie' joining in, their spirits all recovered.

"Will we be able to come over every weekend and play with her?" asked Heather.

"You know you can come over any time you want and the new dog can sleep in your room if you stay over, especially when your Mum and Dad want to have a special weekend together." Joan winked at Mark and Jennifer who smiled at her thankfully.

"Can I give 'Maisie' a biscuit," asked Sean.

"No, but I have some very special treats that she loves and are very good for her, but only give her two each or she won't eat her tea." I went to the cupboard and took down the bag and passed it to Sean who carefully took one out and gave it to 'Maisie' who sat chewing happily, smiling at the two children.

We all stood watching this happy scene, smiling at the joy and happiness that flowed through the room. The scene would've been very different if they knew we had kidnapped this dog and were holding it to ransom, and the loving owners were sitting at home, wringing their hands with worry and grief, tears running down their cheeks as they tried to hold back the fear that they may never see their little 'baby' again. I felt like a proper arsehole, but I kept smiling.

The family stayed for another couple of hours, Joan made sandwiches from the chicken she'd cooked earlier for our lunch, she'd then produced a fruit cake and ice cream for the children, and of course 'Maisie', who apparently also loved ice cream had to have a scoop as well. After more games in the garden, they left with hugs and kisses and promises that we wouldn't get a dog without the children being present at the selection, and that we'd see them next weekend.

The house suddenly felt noticeably quiet and Daisy slumped into her luxurious bed obviously exhausted with all the games and attention lavished on her by the children. We slumped into our armchairs. I didn't say anything about 'our' decision to get a dog, there was plenty of time, a situation was bound to arrive when I needed to use that little 'nugget' of leverage.

CHAPTER 13.

THAT NIGHT I EMAILED instructions to Sheila and Douglas about where and when they were to leave the ransom money. Our plans were the same as when Andrew Johnson had left his blackmail money, behind the gravestone, and we intended to follow the same procedure and level of caution we'd employed on that occasion. One of the downsides to this plan was that we unfortunately had to endure another of Vicar Graham Atkins's Sunday morning services, but it was a small price to pay as we finally drove away from the church with a packet containing the £2000. All that was left to do to conclude the arrangement was to return Daisy, something that I knew Joan felt saddened by as she and the little dog had become friends.

I had originally planned to return Daisy through the hole in the fence of her garden, but I was concerned that the Evans may have repaired it when they discovered Daisy had obviously left by this way. I even thought about taking her back to the churchyard and leaving her tied up behind the gravestone; Joan wasn't happy about this suggestion as she thought Daisy would get distressed being left in a strange place by herself, and she worried someone may steal or kidnap her. I did mention that I couldn't ever imagine anybody doing such a thing!!

In the end we agreed that I would dress up in my 'gentrified landscape gardener' outfit, put Daisy into the pet carrying case, after it had been carefully wiped down to remove any finger prints, drive to the end of the little lane, walk up and leave her and the case, covered with a warm blanket, at the gate, return to the car and as we drove home I would call and tell them where Daisy was. Joan liked this idea as it was the only way that wouldn't distress the dog.

Daisy's return went exactly as we'd planned and that evening we sat feeling pleased another project had worked out successfully, and our financial coffers had been further added to. We both agreed the major lesson we'd learnt was that kidnapping pets for ransom was not a project we would repeat, realising we were no different to all the other 'cutie' dog owners we'd criticised for years; the animals completely took over people's lives, like children, but without any of the childish dramas and petty issues.

The part I found most incredible was Joan, 'Mrs. I can't stand the way people swoon over these ridiculous little animals', who had become one of 'them' herself in the space of a day and was now scouring the countryside, online and logging on to different websites to see what breeders had for sale or were currently breeding. She'd decided to find a dog like Daisy, a Bichon Frise. She collected different photos, attached them to an email to Heather and Sean for their opinion and within minutes they were both on the phone telling her to go ahead and get one, but to let them know immediately it arrives so they could come straight over.

So, apart from concluding that kidnapping pets was not a good idea; too much effort and emotional stress, when balanced against the financial reward, we also discovered a love of little 'cutie' dogs. I was horrified when Joan told me the cost of buying a dog like Daisy was just under a £1000, and then on top of this extortionate amount when all the costs of the petnapping project were added together and set against the £2000 ransom, she thought there would only be enough money left over to buy the dog a pram. This for me was one step too far, I refused ever to be seen out with a dog in a pram, even when Joan pleaded through the voice changer in the little girl voice, promising all sorts of treats, I still refused. "This will never happen." I stated. "I am absolutely certain this will never happen." Well that's what I thought!

CHAPTER 14.

THE ARRIVAL OF 'WOLFIE'; the name the grandchildren decided on, a name that created images of a snarling, powerful creature whose drool dripped to the floor as it looked at you hungrily. This name did not reflect its new owner, as Wolfie was a very small bundle of white fluff with pointy ears, black eyes and nose and a little tail that always wagged happily every time anyone paid it any attention and Heather and Sean certainly gave Wolfie their undivided attention all the time they were with him. Whenever they stayed with us on a Friday or Saturday night, one of their favourite moments was when they were tucked up in bed, with Wolfie in between them, and I told 'made up' stories about the times Wolfie went on great adventures or performed incredible acts of bravery, often by saving someone's life. I just made these stories up by drawing on memories from when I used to watch 'Lassie' on the television when I was a child. Whenever the children took a liking to a particular 'made-up' story, they would ask me to repeat it several days later. Often if the repeat telling was not quite the same as the original, my latest version would be immediately corrected so the story was told exactly as I had told it the time before. One of their absolute favorites was when Wolfie saved the headmaster, Mr. Waverley's life. In the first telling of this story, Wolfie had saved the Postmistresses life, but when Heather said, "What's a Postmistress" we collectively had a discussion about whose life Wolfie should save in the story and they decided it should be their headmaster, Mr. Waverley.

"Once upon a time," every story I told had to start with these four words otherwise it never felt as if a real story was about to start, it seemed to galvanise their attention and everyone, including Wolfie would get themselves thoroughly comfortable. "Once upon a time, on a warm sunny day in the spring when the birds were singing in the trees and the flowers were beginning to burst all over the ground and the bees flew from one bright petal to another, a little dog called," I always paused at this point because the children would shout loudly, 'WOLFIE', "Correct," I'd say. "Wolfie, was trotting along the little path that ran beside the park, he enjoyed this path, seeing the huge trees gently moving in the breeze and the sound of children playing happily on the swings in the playground. As he approached the end of the path where he had to cross the road, he stopped and carefully looked right, then left and then right again, and seeing it was safe walked briskly to the other side. After only a short distance he came to a red telephone box and spotted Mr. Waverley, the headmaster, slumped down on the floor. Wolfie could see that he wasn't very well and barked and barked the words, 'Mr. Waverley, what's wrong?' as he scratched with his front paws against the glass of the door, trying his best to open it so he could begin to use his lifesaving skills to revive Mr. Waverley, but the door wouldn't open. Wolfie quickly realised he would have to run to get help. As he turned to leave he saw that his barking and frantic efforts to help the headmaster had attracted the attention of two of the local 'bully' dogs, they were huge Doberman Pinchers; their shiny black coats rippled with every movement they made, their black eyes glowered at Wolfie as they moved towards him menacingly, they had no interest in helping to save Mr. Waverly, they only wanted to tease and torment Wolfie, they were always bullying him. But this time Wolfie couldn't just cower away and hide as he would normally have done, today he had to help the headmaster who could die if he didn't get help quickly, so he began to run as fast as he could towards the school where he felt sure there would be someone he could tell.

Wolfie's legs were moving so fast they were a blur, he could hear his paws clipping on the pavement like machine gun fire, he could feel his heart pumping in his chest and felt his muscles already beginning to ache, but he pushed even harder as he heard the mocking laughter of the two bully dogs close behind him; one of them said, "Is that as fast as those little ugly stumps of yours can run?" Ha, ha! they laughed, "I'm going to enjoy biting those little legs when I catch you," said the other. Wolfie just kept running and as he turned into a back lane that ran between two rows of houses, he suddenly felt doomed as he looked down the road unable to see anyone who could help him, he knew he wouldn't make it to the end of the lane. His legs were slowing as they became more and more tired, he knew he was only moments away from being caught and hurt by the two big dogs, so with a last effort he barked as loud as he could and shouted, "Help, help, my name is Wolfie and I'm being chased by two bullies. I need to find help to save Mr. Waverley the headmaster who's not very well and is stuck in the phone box. Help, help."

Nothing seemed to change for a few moments as Wolfie tried to drive his aching legs forward, but suddenly a head appeared over the fence and looked over to see what all the commotion was about. The big grey head quickly raised its snout and barked with a deep, thunderous and throaty voice that echoed down the lane announcing. "This is Hector, listen up, Wolfie's in trouble and needs our help, action stations everyone." Suddenly faces appeared over the fences of several houses on both sides of the lane. The first to come to Wolfie's aid was Hector himself, who was a huge Irish hound whose powerful body and long legs soon overtook one of the bullies and using his shoulder he pushed him against a garage door causing him to fall down. When the bully jumped back up, he now faced not only Hector, but also Goldie the pretty Labrador, Jenson the greyhound, Scottie the terrier and Raffles the Corgi. The bully quickly lay down in surrender, very frightened by this powerful collection of Wolfie's friends and was squealing like the coward he was in a high-pitched whimpering voice. "Don't hurt me, we were only having a bit of fun."

Another deep voice barked, "Don't worry Wolfie, you just go and get help for Mr. Waverly, I got this other runt." This deep voice belonged to Rover, a hugely strong bulldog who had easily knocked the second bully to the ground and was standing over him menacingly. "Hector," he barked in his deep voice, "can I chew his ear off?" Wolfie didn't hear any more as he came out of the lane and ran towards the school gate where he saw Heather and Sean. As soon as they saw Wolfie they ran and held him in their arms. "What's wrong Wolfie," they asked, but Wolfie struggled to get his breath back so he could reply. Finally, between gasps he barked as quickly as he could. Heather repeated his story to be sure there was no confusion. "You're saying that on the corner of Park Street, in the telephone box, Mr. Waverley is gravelly unwell and needs help?" "Yes, hurry," replied Wolfie.

Mr. Waverley had been saved and he was very grateful to Wolfie for his great efforts and a grand ceremony was held in the school hall, even the mayor was there with his huge golden chain that showed how important he was. After a short speech by the headmaster, the mayor then presented Wolfie with a medal of honor. They all then enjoyed lashings of ginger beer and peanut butter sandwiches.

It was about this time in the stories that Heather, Sean and Wolfie had fallen asleep and I would go back downstairs considering which bedtime story I would tell them next time; Sean's favorite was

'Wolfie and the Sea Serpents', whereas Heather's joint favorites were 'Wolfie goes Pony Trekking' and 'Wolfie and the Magic Bracelet', but I thought I would invent a new one that would reflect the realism of modern times called, 'Wolfie Captures the Robbers' or 'Wolfie is Kidnapped' or better still 'Wolfie is Knocked Down by a Bus for being such a Fucking Smartass'.

Wolfie, I discovered, brought many other surprising benefits. Obviously we enjoyed having him, particularly Joan who absolutely adored him and we now regularly got to spend lots of time with our grandchildren who came around most weekends to play with the dog; or we went to their house, with the dog; or we went to their school sports events, with the dog. But there were other benefits to support our 'professional' careers. We bought Wolfie a pram. I know I vowed to never ever consider walking around pushing a dog in a pram, but I quickly realised that everyone stops to talk to you and admire Wolfie; you get to know so many people who are happy to tell you where they live, what's going on in their lives and how they were thinking about getting a dog themselves. Nobody would ever suspect a gentle, elderly couple pushing a pram with a cute little dog in it called Wolfie, of spying and planning to rob them!

So, it was with Wolfie's help that we managed over the next few months to accumulate a lot of cash from two more blackmailing projects and three additional cash point 'heists.' The latest 'heist' is here at the Armstrong's house, where I sit in an armchair, wearing my balaclava while watching Mr. Armstrong, who continues to sit quietly in his own armchair opposite.

After all my dreamlike 'thoughts and reflections', I'm left feeling unexpectedly confused. I feel so tired and a comatose, lethargic state seems to be consuming me. I'm finding it very difficult to stop thinking of the memories, circumstances and events that have all conspired to bring me to this moment, but I'm suddenly no longer sure what the realities of this moment are.

I begin to worry once again where Joan is; she's been away a long time, too long to follow the plans we'd made. I'm not sure of exactly what the time is now, or how long she's actually been away. I just feel so tired, I can't even open my eyes to find out. I think I can still feel the comfort of the chair, and the warmth from the fire, and hear the irritating clock, but oddly, as I listen carefully, I think the 'tick tock' seems much slower than it had been earlier, and I sense my shallow breath and beating heart are following its declining rhythm.

I feel even more confused; I'm no longer certain of where I am. Strangely, I'm beginning to believe that if I did open my eyes I would see Joan beside me, but I know this isn't possible as there's not enough room on the armchair for both of us. I decide we must be lying in our bed together at home. I imagine seeing her gentle, half closed eyes looking back at me with love, and her mouth offering a faint smile. I smile back to reassure her of my love, the moment feels everlasting, she seems so peaceful and still. I can't hear or feel her breath anymore, but I feel no panic, only peace.

In this deep soporific state, a small corner of my mind struggles to understand. Was this moment lying next to Joan in our bed a dream? Or was the ticking clock and the warm seat in front of the fire in Mr. Armstrong's house a dream? I wasn't very sure which 'reality' was the dream.

I imagine that if I am lying in bed next to Joan, we must have decided that life wasn't worth fighting for and taken the sleeping tablets we'd acquired. Was this calm tranquility my last moments before death? Had all the planning and our exploits of blackmail, theft, petnapping, and everything else just been an imaginary dream of what might have happened had we lived? I wanted to tell Joan how great things could've been and how our lives didn't need to end in this sad way, lying side by side in bed. The darkness closed in and I heard my breath slow further to match the distant sound of the beating clock.

CHAPTER 15.

"WAKE UP." I felt the hand of God gently rocking me from side to side. "Wake up." God demanded, more forcibly and impatiently this time. I wondered what heaven would look like when I opened my eyes; would it be filled with cherubim and seraphim flying about flapping their little golden wings and playing harps; I couldn't hear any music though, just a distant voice. I wondered if there would be any cute little dogs like Wolfie or Daisy in heaven, I felt certain there would be. I imagined St. Peter holding a set of scales with a feather on one side and a questionnaire for me to fill in on the other. I wondered if Joan had arrived, what if she wasn't there and she'd been sent to the other place; I really hoped she would be standing there with an angelic, loving and welcoming smile to greet me with adoration.

"WAKE UP," the voice shouted, sounding annoyed and very loud to the extent that it made me immediately open my eyes. Joan was standing there, but not with an angelic welcoming face full of love and adoration, this was a face covered in a black knitted balaclava with two blood shot tired eyes staring back at me.

"Oh, sorry about that," I explained, "I just closed my eyes for a moment." I noticed that it now felt quite cool since the fire in the grate had long since burnt out, I could also see that the clock read 1.15am and Mr. Armstrong remained sitting in the opposite armchair. "I was…" Joan put her finger over my lips to stop me saying anything further; I remembered I was on a 'mission' and not supposed to speak unless there was an emergency. Where her fingers pressed the balaclava against the skin at the side of my mouth, I realised it was sodden and decided I must have been drooling in the depth of my slumber; a sleep that although had now completely vanished, the dreams and reflections still held me in a tight embrace and left a confusion and strange longing lingering in my soul, however I was pleased this was reality, I would've been disappointed if Joan and I had chosen the other 'path'.

Joan leant over and whispered in my ear. "Are you Ok and fully awake?" I nodded as she continued. "A number of the local ATM's weren't working or had run out of cash, so we had to travel a long way to get what we wanted and rather than coming all the way back here to travel back out there again, Olivia and I waited in a supermarket car park until midnight had passed before we repeated the exercise in reverse."

"Olivia? You're on first name terms now?" I asked, more than a little surprised.

"I discovered she's a really nice person and since we spent so much time together, we got talking about ourselves and our problems. I briefly explained our circumstances."

"You told her our circumstances?" I whispered a little too loudly and abruptly in my surprise. Joan put her finger back over my mouth to silence me again, her eyes glancing over at Mr. Armstrong who continued to sit perfectly still as if he was straining to hear what we were talking about.

"I only explained to her briefly why we'd been driven to do what we're doing; I didn't give away who we are or any details she could identify us with. Anyway, once she had this explanation, she was very sympathetic and helpful. She also confided in me that things for her had become extremely difficult, particularly over the past year as her husband, Gerald." Joan paused for a second to again glance over at Mr. Armstrong as if to introduce us on first name terms. "He had become quite violent towards her, apparently he'd hurt her on many different occasions throughout their marriage, nothing serious enough to require treatment, but enough to cause her bruising and pain to her ribs and back. She showed me some of the purply blue and yellow bruising to her upper arms. Poor woman." Joan paused for a moment reflecting on her conversation.

"When she was telling me this it was as if she'd finally found someone she could tell or confess to, someone that couldn't ever repeat her confession, and I obviously couldn't ever say anything to anyone. Then she told me that Gerald had been diagnosed with early stage dementia shortly after they were married, just over five years ago. He'd immediately had problems at work with his colleagues and eventually lost his job; with his age and declining mental health, he'd found it very difficult to find anything useful to occupy himself. With his growing frustration he had increasingly taken out his anger on her. She was so upset and cried so hard as we sat in the car, I couldn't do anything but hold her and offer some sympathetic comfort, it made our circumstances seem very superficial. They are the complete opposite to us; we have all the happiness but no money, they have plenty of money but are desperately unhappy."

"Where is she now?" I whispered.

"In the kitchen making some tea. I think before she comes back, we ought to take the sack off Mr. Armstrong's head so he can drink his. For the sake of our continued role play as ruthless robbers, will you point your gun at him, he'll not cause any trouble since we'll keep his hands and feet tied, but for Olivia's sake we want to keep up appearances."

"Did you get any money between all these bouts of female confession and emotional outbursts?" I whispered, but failed to get a reply as Mrs. Armstrong, Olivia entered the room carrying a tray, which she put on the table. I could see that there was an elegant bone china tea pot with four matching cups and saucers, milk jug and sugar bowl. I instantly liked this woman; even though she had been threatened with guns, trailed around the countryside and robbed by a pair of masked thieves while her husband had suffered the indignity of being tied up in a chair with a sack over his head, there on the tea tray was a matching china, three levelled cake stand ladened with little finger cucumber sandwiches, a selection of biscuits, some

Dundee cake, my favorite, and four fruit scones with a pot of strawberry jam. How had she done this, even Joan looked on with amazement as she finished loosening the draw strings that held the sack on Mr. Armstrong's head and pulled it off.

Joan stepped back expecting his head to snap up and his mouth to start spouting complaints and insults, we were all more than a little surprised to see a very pale face and two staring, unfocused eyes glowering back at us. None of us moved. Joan was frozen to the spot with the sack hanging from her hand, I sat with the plastic toy gun pointing directly at the swollen purple tongue that protruded from his mouth. Olivia was stooped over the china cups about to pour the tea. The only sound that existed in the room was the irritating tick tock of the clock on the mantle shelf. We just continued to stare at the dead corpse that was Mr. Armstrong, Gerald to his friends, sitting in his armchair.

In those frozen moments, my mind flew through our options, and like a computer in overdrive I began preparing a list of actions, in order of preference and priority, to protect Joan and myself: -

Option 1 – Get up out of the chair, grab Joan and get the fuck out of the house, get back to our car, drive home, have a large whiskey and agree never ever to talk about this unfortunate incident again.

I even reviewed what evidence we may have left in the house or in Olivia's car that a forensic person could find and lead to our identity, I could think of nothing; both of us had been rigorous in ensuring that we wouldn't make such errors. I hoped!

Option 2 – Get up out of the chair, grab Joan and get the fuck out of the house…. I couldn't think of another option, the first was the only sensible and safe action to follow.

Things in the room began to come back to life, slowly. I started to push myself out of the armchair, Olivia put the milk jug down, spilling a great deal of the contents in the process and Joan began to take off her black, handknitted balaclava.

"Joan, what are you doing?" I suddenly realised my error by using her name and giving away her identity. She turned quickly towards me, obviously annoyed at my foolish error and went to correct me.

"Brian, we agreed…" She stopped, realising she'd made the same mistake in this moment of stress. I couldn't help but smile as I remembered a scene from the TV series of 'Dad's Army' when the

German officer demanded young Pike's name and Captain Mannering had quickly stopped him with the order, 'Don't tell him Pike!" A smile spread across Joan's face, she must have read my thoughts, but continued to remove her balaclava, throwing it into our bag.

Everything in the room again stilled as I began once again to review our options, which had suddenly become much more complicated: -

Option 1 – Get up out of the chair, leave Joan staring at Mr. Armstrong and get the fuck out of the house, get back to the car, drive home, have a large whisky and pretend, when asked, that I had no idea what my wife had been doing all evening.

Option 2 – Get up out of the chair, pick up the heavy cast iron poker from the fireplace, walk over and beat Olivia to death, grab Joan, get the fuck out of the house, get back to our car, drive home, have a large whisky and agree never to mention this sad event ever again.

I decided that much of the contents of my review process were repetitive, so I concentrated on the major headline variations.

Option 3 – Same as option 2 but setting fire to the house as we left.

Option 4 – Take Olivia hostage and keep her locked up at a place somewhere that I couldn't immediately think of, until something else happened that I also couldn't immediately think of.

I realised that all these options were neither plausible or practical, and more than hinted at hysteria; the reality of the situation was that Joan and I were inseparable partners and Option 1 would never happen, and so I took off my balaclava as well, which caused both women to look over in my direction.

"Is he dead?" Asked Olivia in a hesitant whisper.

"I never touched him," I whined in a rapid schoolgirl croak, "I did loosen the cord that tied his hands a little and the string holding the sack over his head when he complained they were too tight, but I didn't do anything else, I didn't kill him." I heard my voice rising to even higher soprano levels as I tried to reassure Olivia and Joan, who both continued to stare at me accusingly.

Olivia walked over and touched her husband's face, she then knelt in front of him and removed the cords from his wrists and ankles, took his hands in hers, lowered her head and began to weep. Joan went over and knelt beside her, placing her arm around Olivia's shoulders to comfort her.

"I am so sorry." Joan said.

I didn't know what to do. Should I pour the tea, it would be a shame to let it go cold, so I stood and walked over to the tray and completed the task that Olivia had begun by putting milk in the cups and pouring the tea. I didn't like to interrupt the grieving by asking Olivia if she took sugar, I just quietly and reverentially took my own, helping myself to a couple of sandwiches, a slice of Dundee cake and a scone, with a good helping of strawberry jam. I sat back down and began to munch.

Although I was very hungry I did try to eat politely and with respect to the situation going on over at the other armchair, unfortunately the room was so quiet, apart from the ticking clock, that every time I bit into the food and attempted to chew, the sound of me eating seemed to be incredibly loud; I even tried taking little nibbles and then sucking it rather than chewing, but this seemed to generate a different and rather unpleasant sound effect that had both women turning to glower at me once again. I stopped chewing and looked back at them sympathetically, and thoughtfully asked.

"Would you like some tea." I assumed they obviously didn't as Joan completely ignored me and turned to Olivia and suggested.

"I think we should call an ambulance."

"And probably the Police." I added, a few crumbs spraying out of my mouth to support the words. Both women stood up and Joan helped Olivia to a seat on the sofa before taking a blanket and spreading it over Gerald; I felt I could call him by his first name now, recognizing that the time for social formalities had probably passed.

"I think I'd like to just sit quietly before we contact anyone and everything becomes 'difficult'. Would you both stay with me for a while?" Requested Olivia.

"I think we must stay and explain to the police why we're here; I don't know why this has happened to your husband, but we obviously must take some responsibility. It's likely that the stress of us threatening him with our 'guns' before tying him up and blindfolding him may have caused, or at least attributed to his…" Joan stopped, she couldn't seem to be able to say the word 'death' for fear of upsetting Olivia. Silence again descended over the room. I looked longingly at the plate of unfinished sandwiches and cakes, feeling slightly aggrieved that I would never again get the opportunity of eating tasty morsels like this, I sensed that from now on it would be little more than rancid water and stale bread.

Suddenly Olivia took Joan's hand. "I have something I must tell you." She paused as she looked down at their entwinned hands, seeming to struggle over what she wanted to say. "It may be true that you being here tonight and the things you've done could have advanced Gerald's death, but he was going to die tonight anyway," she paused as if considering whether she should continue, finally whispering, "because I poisoned him." Joan and I stared at Olivia, it was obvious, again, that neither of us could think of what to say; this was an unexpected confession, a complete shock that changed everything. Up until this moment I'd just assumed Gerald's death was entirely Joan and my fault, and I'd already been preparing myself, in my mind, for a lengthy incarceration in prison.

"The reason I'm telling you this," continued Olivia, "is because we would all be held responsible in differing degrees if the police became involved. I couldn't believe how lucky I was when you arrived to rob us tonight, tying Gerald up before taking me away so I couldn't see him die. I can't thank you both enough, particularly you Joan for listening to me and showing such thoughtful kindness and sympathy. I believed in my heart that if I'd had to sit and watch him, I would probably have been too weak and called an ambulance, saving him by confessing what I'd done. So, he probably wouldn't have died had you not arrived." Olivia concluded before continuing.

"The problem now though, is that the three of us have become connected and jointly responsible; we've each played a part in Gerald's death. None of us want to call an ambulance or the police; the price we would all likely pay is a lengthy jail sentence." She paused, her brow creased in thought. "I don't have any ideas or plan of what we should do next, my only suggestion is that we have a drink to calm our nerves and help us concentrate." Olivia got up and without any choice being offered, poured out and handed us a large glass of whisky each. Joan and I looked at each other, the confusion and fear I felt was reflected in her face. I felt that somehow Olivia had manipulated this situation and set us up, but how could she have done when it had been us who had planned out all the details of this event and allowed, as we thought, for every eventuality? Neither of us could immediately think of what to say, either to each other or to Olivia as she sat back down on the sofa next to Joan and we sipped our drinks.

As my mind cleared it began its usual process of producing different options. The first, of calling for the Police and an ambulance could not now be considered. I therefore fell back on earlier ideas, now with a few extra details: – *'Get up out of the chair, pick up the heavy cast iron poker from the fireplace, walk over and beat Olivia to death. Wash the dishes and tidy up, put the rest of the sandwiches, cake and scones in a bag to eat later, grab Joan, get out of the house, get back to our car, drive home, have another large whisky and agree never to mention this sad incident ever again'*. The problem I realised with this idea was that the Police would obviously know there had been some 'foul play' and would begin a 'manhunt', again I feared that no matter how careful we'd been, an intensive investigation would eventually result in us being caught.

To avoid this situation, I reasoned, instead of killing Olivia here in the house we could take her hostage, drive her car out to a cliff somewhere and throw her off so it looked like a suicide brought about by grief and despair because she'd poisoned and killed her husband. We would unfortunately have to leave the money in her car in case the police looked at their bank balances and wondered why she'd taken out a large amount of cash that evening, why she did this would just have to remain an unsolved mystery for them. Could Joan and I cold bloodily throw Olivia off a cliff? This was the question I pondered in my imagination as I visualised Olivia fighting for her life; clawing, biting, punching, and screaming as we tried to get her over the cliff edge. No, I thought, we'd never manage that, we'd have to knock her out at the house first so we could get her in the car and then throw her off the cliff with no ungainly hysterics.

I brought my thoughts back to reality, recognizing that these imaginings were purely academic; in reality Joan and I couldn't kill her or even hurt her. I had even come to admire the woman in a strange sort of way; the fact she had decided to kill her husband showed her strength of mind, and she was obviously a kind person at heart since she'd made some lovely food to keep us going, but most importantly, Joan and her seemed to have become quite good friends. I therefore considered it very unlikely I would receive any help from Joan to kill Olivia, and I certainly couldn't do it by myself. The problem was there didn't seem to be a single scenario that provided a solution to our situation that involved keeping Olivia alive. I reflected that our lives may have lacked great excitement before our retirement, and we'd certainly never done anything that could've prepared us for this situation, but at this moment I would happily have swapped back to our earlier boring lives, even if it meant living in squalid poverty!

"What did you poison Gerald with?" I asked to break the long, uncomfortable silence that had descended upon us as we drank our whisky. She looked at me and smiled.

"I used to be a chemist in one of my first husband's shops." She explained; her stated profession implying that preparing a 'killer' concoction would not have been difficult for her. The silence returned and my thoughts once again considered our dilemma, I tried to look at the problem in a different way. If we weren't going to kill Olivia, our only other option was to get rid of

Gerald and the three of us agree to somehow support and protect each other and prevent the truth of what happened here tonight emerging. A quite odd but simple plan began to form in my mind and when I looked up I realised that both Olivia and Joan were staring at me; I wondered if I'd been thinking aloud and attracted their attention, or had they been speaking to me and I hadn't heard since I was so focused on my thoughts.

"What do you think we should do?" I asked and realised I hadn't missed out on anything as their responses were simply shrugs and blank looks.

"I have a suggestion," I continued, their interest immediately captured. "Since we all seem to have a level of responsibility for Gerald's death, we therefore have a shared interest in avoiding the truth being known to the police, which as we know would likely result in us being arrested and imprisoned. My suggestion is that we write out an honest and accurate account of exactly what's happened here tonight. Olivia, you must state why and how you poisoned him, and then further explain that you quickly began to have feelings of remorse and were going to summon help to save him, but were prevented from doing so because we arrived and restrained you. We should however state that at no time did you tell us you'd poisoned your husband, so we couldn't have known. We for our part of this statement, will admit to imprisoning and attempting to rob by forcing you to go to cash machines to withdraw money. We can then conclude by detailing how we discovered that Gerald was dead, and our subsequent joint decision to dispose of his body without notifying the authorities.

If we prepare a document setting out these events as a true record, print out an additional copy and all sign them, we can at least then feel a little more confident that none of us are going to report the other to the police. What do you think?"

"I think it's a good idea," agreed Olivia, "at least it gives us a basis to work together to resolve the situation." She paused. "I want you both to know that in a strange way I'm pleased he's dead and I'm grateful to you both for preventing me from changing my mind."

"Agreeing a statement of tonight's events is good, but what does it really achieve?" asked Joan, "Gerald is still dead and is still sitting in his chair, what do we do with him? I can't think of anything other than calling an ambulance to take him away, and then, irrespective of any 'agreement' we will all suffer the consequences." She looked between Olivia and me in turn, her hands turned up questioningly. Olivia shrugged her shoulders again.

"Well," I paused, trying to think of how best to explain my proposal, "the only solution that doesn't involve calling the authorities, and this does sounds really crazy, is that we put him in the car, drive to our house and bury him in our garden."

"What!" exclaimed Joan sounding shocked, "why would we need to do that? Why can't we just bury him here in his own garden at the back of the house?"

"At some point quite soon," I explained, "Olivia will have to report Gerald as missing. I'm certain that when he hasn't turned up or been found after a certain period, they will begin to suspect 'foul play' and that Olivia may be responsible in some way for his disappearance. They will probably then arrange for both the house and garden to be searched and will quickly discover his body and then we'll all be in even more trouble. We could try to get rid of his body in some other way or place, but the same problem exists if his body is found. It would be extremely difficult for us to dig a grave in some remote spot without it looking suspicious and being reported. However, we can dig a grave in our garden, I was thinking right at the end beside the compost heap where none of our neighbours can see us. Why would anybody ever think of looking in our garden for Gerald?"

"I can understand why you've suggested this," interrupted Joan, "but it is definitely not going to happen, I love our house and I could never sit in the garden again knowing that Gerald was there, he'd keep haunting me." She shivered, "No, we've got to think of somewhere else or somebody else's garden."

"Like who or where?" I asked, noticing that Olivia was watching and listening intently as Joan and I debated the final resting place for her husband, she didn't seem to care and showed little enthusiasm to interrupt our debate with a suggestion of her own.

Joan thought for a minute. "Well, before we decided to rob Olivia and Gerald, we considered robbing those people beside the railway station. Their garden looked quite big, we could go there and repeat everything we've done here tonight, except avoiding any deaths. While I'm away getting the money you and Olivia can dig a grave in their garden and when I come back, we could then bury Gerald."

We sat silently for a few minutes before I couldn't help but laugh out loud at how ridiculous her suggestion sounded. The thought of us turning up with our balaclavas, (which we'd have to buy for Olivia as Joan wouldn't have time to knit her a 'made to measure' one), plus gloves and dark 'criminal' clothes, our cardboard 'false' delivery box, toy guns, spades, shovels and Gerald's body in a wheelbarrow, all while holding people hostage and committing a robbery seemed to me to be hilariously funny. Unfortunately, neither Joan or Olivia saw the vision I'd seen and looked at me with unamused faces. After giving me a final stern look, Olivia turned her attention back to Joan to show her solidarity and that she at least was taking the situation seriously.

"I have a friend down the road whose husband died earlier this year, he had prostrate cancer, they were very close and she's still grieving, poor soul. I've been meaning to call her and take her out for a meal to give her a little treat and some company. She's still living in the family house but has recently put it up for sale as it's too big for her, and she says it constantly reminds her of her loss. Her garden is huge and very private, we could easily bury Gerald there. I could take her out for dinner one evening while you two bury him."

"That sounds a much better idea," agreed Joan. "Brian and I could probably dig a grave, but I think it'll take all three of us to get Gerald from the car and I'm sure you'll want to be present when he's buried." Joan looked compassionately at Olivia who I thought was going to say that she wasn't particularly bothered, instead she nodded her head in agreement.

"Yes, of course, you're right." She paused, looking over at the shrouded form that was her husband, her thoughts perhaps trying to imagine how she would feel and what she might like to say as she helped bury him. Her moment of reflection passed, and she returned to her more practical self. "I think we should put Gerald into the boot of his car tonight, then tomorrow I'll arrange to take Jaqueline, my friend, out for the evening and you can go over with the wheelbarrow, spades and all the equipment, dig the grave and then leave. When I come back and drop her off, I can wait and watch for when she's gone to bed, come back to get Gerald's car and then we can bury Gerald together."

"That sounds OK." I agreed with some hesitation, I hated when things were not planned in minute detail and this all sounded a bit casual and improvised. "Just a couple of things. Firstly, we'll have to go around to your friend's house now and look at her garden, you know, how do we get access and choose the best place to dig the grave type of things?"

"What now?" interrupted Joan, "it's nearly 3.00am!"

"I think Brian's right Joan, it'll not be much earlier when we go tomorrow night to bury Gerald, and there isn't really any other time we could safely go over and work out the details of how we do this. I've got some black clothes upstairs; I'll get changed and then we can go." Olivia was getting up to leave when I stopped her by asking some other questions.

"What about Gerald's car? When you report him missing to the police and you explain how you'd gone out to get some cash, as he'd asked you to, and how when you returned after midnight for the second time, he'd left. Can you explain why he wanted you to get this money? Why didn't he wait for you to return with the second lot of cash? How did he leave since his car is still parked in the garage?"

Olivia sat back down. "Shit, I never gave those things any thought and I don't know what the answers are." She looked fraught and a little anxious for almost the first time during this whole evening of farcical trauma. Joan again took her hands sympathetically.

"My suggestion would be that we deal with one thing at a time. Right now, after you've got changed, we should go over to your friend's house to plan how to do things tomorrow night and then return here, put Gerald into the boot of his car and complete our agreements and then we go home to bed. Tomorrow night we'll have plenty of time to work out the solution to those other minor details, I'm sure there will be plenty of other things we haven't yet thought of that will be apparent after a nights sleep, so go and get changed Olivia." Joan instructed authoritatively.

After she'd gone upstairs, I turned to Joan and whispered.

"I don't particularly like this plan and I'm definitely not sure if we can trust her, with or without an agreement. I know we made a promise not to hurt anyone, but this situation is completely out of control and very risky for us. I believe we should hit her over the head, put her into our car, drive down to the old quarry with both cars and throw her over. We then leave her car, and everyone will believe she's committed suicide after killing her husband. It's our safest option."

"Brian, we can't do that, what's happened here tonight is bad enough, but to kill Olivia and throw her body into the quarry is too coldblooded, I couldn't do it and I don't think you could either. All three of us are in this together and if we complete our agreement and all sign it when we come back from checking out this friend's garden, everything should be alright. I think we can trust her, she's in much more trouble than we are if this comes out. Let's just get these things done and then we can go home."

We stopped our whispered conversation as we heard Olivia returning down the stairs, when she entered the room I was surprised how different she looked; gone were the baggy, grey 'jogging' outfit she'd been wearing to accompany Joan to the cash point machines, now she wore smart, tailored black trousers, an elegant black shirt and a large black scarf that she carefully wrapped around her neck and over her head; not quite as 'criminal' a disguise as our balaclava's, but adequate for tonight.

I realised Olivia had caught me staring at her shapely figure, but as I looked up and our eyes met, I saw the biggest change in her. No longer did she appear tired, lonely and defeated, she now looked bright, determined and even mischievous; her husband's death seemed to have had the opposite effect to what I'd expected, it was obvious she was relieved he was no longer around to threaten and control her.

"Are you alright Joan," she asked, "you mustn't worry, everything will work out for the best." I saw the surprised look on Joan's face as Olivia asked her this question with such a level of care and compassion; it felt like a complete role reversal.

"Yes, I'm fine, just still upset and shocked at Gerald's death and our plans to dispose of him without any ceremony or the involvement of any authorities. I feel sad." Olivia walked over and held Joan in an effort to reassure her. I noticed that despite feeling a little anxious myself I wasn't offered any of the physical comforts that Joan received. I decided it was time for me to show my authority and take control of the situation since Joan seemed to have suddenly become the 'victim'.

"Come on, let's go and check out your friend's garden." I said, standing up to emphasise my instruction.

"In a moment," replied Olivia briskly, "can't you see your wife's upset?" I couldn't immediately think of a reply but remained standing, feeling a little foolish while Joan and Olivia comforted each other.

When they finally stood up to leave, it was Olivia that led us out of the house to her car, directing Joan to the front passenger seat and leaving me, feeling like some miscreant, to sit in the back. She drove out of the driveway turning right on the road, but for only a short distance as she then made a series of left and right turnings before slowing and switching off the headlights to enter the drive of a large house where she silently pulled up to the side. I tried to memorise exactly the route from Olivia's house to here so I would find it tomorrow night, but since it was very dark and she hadn't made it easy for me to follow, I decided to make a special effort on the return journey.

Olivia was first out of the car and Joan and I followed her to a side gate.

"Jaqueline never locks this gate; I keep telling her that it's an open invitation to a burglar." She whispered, pushing at the gate which opened with what seemed to our supercharged senses like a deafening creak. We stood absolutely still, listening for any sounds from the house and watching for a light to be switched on, but all remained still and dark; I vowed to bring some WD40 with me to oil the hinges tomorrow night. "Follow me," she explained, "I know the path, so we won't have to use our torches until we get to the bottom of the garden and out of sight from the house." We silently moved on down a hardened path bordered by small box hedging. I don't know why but we all crouched low like pantomime crooks as we crept along; I'm sure if we'd just walked normally we would've been much quieter, looked far less suspicious and my back and legs wouldn't have been aching. We finally reached a huge hedge where our path turned a sharp right and ran parallel, separated by what looked in the darkness to be a border garden of roses. We reached an opening in the hedge, which formed an archway and we went through continuing along the path, still maintaining our ridiculous cartoon style walk. I sensed we'd entered a vegetable garden and the hedge had been the boundary between what was the formal flower gardens and lawns and this 'working' end of the garden. I realised that Olivia hadn't exaggerated when she said this garden was huge. She suddenly stopped, and I bumped into the back of Joan who had to take hold of Olivia to stop herself from falling over.

"Sorry," I said and was immediately blinded as Olivia turned her torch on and pointed it at my face.

"Brian, where do you think would be best to dig a grave?" She asked as if I was some sort of specialist, while in fact I had no real idea of where I was and all I could see was the image of the torch light which had burnt an impression on my eyes. I stood quietly for a moment pretending that I was considering my answer when I was really trying to recover. I finally turned my torch on and allowed the light to explore the area. I could see several fruit trees to the right of the path and assumed that area was a small orchard; I decided that trying to dig there with the likelihood of extensive tree roots would not be sensible. My torch light began to explore the left hand side of the path and I could immediately see this area had been well cultivated in the past; there were still rotten Brussel sprout plants that had been left standing like eerily shaped stalagmites, areas of weeds that had begun to grow where potatoes had been dug up, and then there was a line where somebody, the gardener presumably, had begun to work the soil in preparation for replanting.

"I think just here would be best because hopefully there won't be any tree roots and the ground would still look as if it was being prepared for replanting like the rest of the area and shouldn't raise any suspicion after we've finished." I explained confidently, shining my torch directly into Olivia's face to indicate that I was talking to her, and as a childish act of revenge.

Having agreed this decision, we made our way back up the garden path, back through the side gate, which again creaked as we opened and shut it, into the car and drove back in silence to Olivia's house to finalise our written agreement. This document was not difficult to write, it was Joan who acted as scribe whilst Olivia and I provided the commentary, and as bizarre as the written record appeared, it was simply a true reflection of the events that had happened in the past eight hours, a period of time that had seemed like days.

We read the document through carefully, took a photocopy using Gerald's copier in his well-equipped home office and we all signed them both.

Unfortunately, with this task done there was nothing left for us to do but the grisly task of moving Gerald's body from the armchair and into the boot of his car.

I think we all suspected this was not going to be either a pleasant or an easy task, but none of our imaginings could've prepared us for just how difficult and upsetting it was. Firstly, we had to prise him out of the chair; 'prise' was the only description possible as he was rigidly 'frozen' into a sitting position, rigor mortis having set his arms, legs, body and facial features into this position that looked natural when he was sat in the chair, but very bizarre when we levered him forward and he landed on the blanket we had spread out on the floor. It was his knees that hit the floor first, I almost expected him to raise his hands to stop his face hitting the floor next, but they remained resting in his lap. And there he lay as if he was praying to Mecca with his heals and arse sticking up in the air. I wished I could've taken a picture of Gerald's poise and the three of us standing around looking down at him with horrified expressions on our faces, it was certainly one of those 'once in a lifetime' memories that remains burnt into your memory for all time. For all the moment was very traumatic, once the initial shock had passed, I nearly burst out laughing and had to turn my face away from the scene to disguise my exceptionally poor taste in humour.

As we recovered some of our composure, and for Gerald's dignity, we lay him on his side, his staring eyes and grim feature glowering at us malevolently as we dragged, pushed, pulled and twisted him until we finally had him in the garage and at the rear of his car with the boot lid open. We tried to work out if he would even fit and debated for some time as to which position would accommodate him best, finally deciding that his back end and legs should go in first, we could then turn him so his face would slide under the inside edge of the boot opening.

Gerald wasn't a big man, but it took all our efforts to lift him up and slide him into the car, and all went as planned except we had to force his legs together in order to close the lid. Finally, at 5.30 am, having agreed the arrangements for the following evening with Olivia, Joan and I drove home, completely exhausted and went to bed.

CHAPTER 16.

I HAD TOUGHT WE WOULD go straight to sleep, and this was the case for Joan who, within minutes was snoring lightly into her pillow. As soon as I settled however, my mind went into overdrive, despite my exhaustion it would not rest as it reviewed the evening's events. I smiled occasionally in wonder at how a normal, mature, retired couple could ever have got themselves into such a predicament. I began to wrestle with the conundrum of how to make it appear that Gerald had simply left Olivia and disappeared; where could he have gone? Why had he gone with only a small amount of cash? Where should his car be left to support the belief that he had disappeared? I also began to worry that despite our caution we hadn't been careful enough when wrapping Gerald's body before we put it in the boot, maybe evidence could be found that he'd been put there. I began rehearsing how we were going to get his awkwardly shaped corpse back out of the boot and just as I was concluding that we'd probably have to break his legs, I fell asleep.

I was aware that I tossed and turned, waking myself up several times. I finally awoke with the sun streaming through the sides of the curtains that were drawn across the windows, Joan still slept soundly as I looked across at the clock which told me it was 10.30 am. I lay quietly, again thinking of what had happened and what lay ahead; one thing that my mind wouldn't let go of was Olivia. I remembered how I'd found her physically attractive when she'd returned after changing into her 'criminal' outfit, even though the circumstances for those thoughts to even occur were inappropriate. I wondered why I found her attractive, was it the traumatic situation that had pushed us together or how we all now found ourselves in a partnership of deception and criminality? She'd certainly made no effort to encourage these base thoughts, in fact quite the opposite, most of the time she treated me with contempt, often ignoring any suggestions I made, and when she did acknowledge me, her response always seemed to be abrupt. Out of choice she obviously preferred to speak with Joan and I usually heard Olivia's thoughts, opinions and comments as a third-party bystander. It was apparent that she had a great fondness for Joan, the two women appeared to have genuinely formed a bond of friendship, a rapidly growing union that I was excluded from; I felt certain that Olivia disliked me, her whole demeanor seemed to ooze feelings of contempt; I wondered if these feelings were personal solely to me or if she held the same feeling towards all men. I decided that when an appropriate moment arrived, I would speak to Joan and see what she thought.

I continued to lie in bed quietly, not wanting to disturb Joan who continued to sleep soundly. My mind soon returned to the questions that had kept me awake, how to convince the world that Gerald had left Olivia of his own volition and disappeared? The many ideas that had raced through my tired mind earlier resurfaced. What would happen if after we buried Gerald, we did little else; Olivia didn't report him missing to the police, she just pretended to friends and neighbours that he was away on business? How long would it be before someone noticed he was missing? Who was likely to notice he was missing? Did Olivia and Gerald have any family? Did Gerald work and if so, who were his work colleagues or clients? I needed to find out answers to all these questions from Olivia because I decided it may be best to do nothing, apart from cleaning and parking Gerald's car somewhere. Olivia could simply state, when she had to eventually explain, that Gerald had up and left her; could anyone after a period of time prove otherwise? I decided that if I asked Olivia these questions she would likely treat them with suspicion and irritation, but if I talked them through with Joan, explaining the 'do nothing option' and she then asked these questions I imagined her answers would be much more fruitful and productive to help develop a solution that would explain her apparent ignorance of what had happened to Gerald.

I considered that after burying Gerald we drive his car to some remote place where there were no CCTV cameras and park it, returning in either ours or Olivia's car. She could then leave it for say a week or two before contacting the police to report him missing, if the car wasn't found before then.

A further thought had occurred to me that may have some importance, I wondered if Gerald had any life insurance policies that Olivia might depend on receiving to support her now he wasn't around; I felt certain that when someone simply went missing it could be several years before policies released any payments. A large insurance policy could also be considered a motive for a crime. I needed to know more about Olivia's financial situation to discover if she may have some difficulties. Again, I decided to brief Joan and get her to have that conversation as well.

I still believed we should've killed Olivia by throwing her off the quarry edge to make it look like suicide after she'd apparently killed Gerald, I should've been more assertive with Joan at the time, however, it was too late to exercise that option now, but I did try to invent another plan that would result in Olivia's death and give Joan and I full peace of mind. I realised that any plan involving, I paused my thoughts as I suddenly realised the word that came next was 'murder'; I don't know why it suddenly occurred to me that killing Olivia in cold blood was 'murder', it sounded awful, so premeditated, I'd never ever considered 'murdering' someone before, when I'd thought about killing Olivia earlier, it was somehow an act of self defence, a means of protecting our liberty, an unplanned situation that was an acceptable solution to an unfortunate event we had no control over; she was after all the real killer in this situation and her death was a natural consequence. However, to actually plan her death and kill her was murder; I would become a 'murderer'. Could I do such a thing and live the rest of my life reliving the details of what I'd done. I wasn't sure, so I ran through in my mind an imaginary scenario to see how I felt: -

I imagined that after the three of us had buried Gerald, we could drop Joan off at our house, since there was no point in all three of us driving for miles to a remote place out in the countryside to leave Gerald's car. After we arrived, which I visualized as being a car park beside a wood in a large country park type of place, Olivia would park Gerald's car and begin to get out with the intention of locking it up and joining me in her car, which I had driven up and planned to return home in. However, I quickly got out of the car and armed with a wheel brace I rushed over and stood beside her car as she climbed out. I could see her face as a surprised look crossed her fine features, a look that changed to fear as she saw the weapon held above my head ready to strike. Finally, her look turned to sadness and longing for what might have existed between us.

In my mind I paused the descent of my intended killer blow as I suddenly felt confused with the look I'd imagined seeing on her face. Why would I consider seeing a look of, 'longing'? After some thought I realised 'longing' wasn't the right word, 'desire' was better; did I believe in my subconscious that Olivia's attitude towards me was to disguise her feelings of 'desire' for me? It was suddenly obvious, I realised that Olivia didn't desire me in any lustful way, she desired the relationship that Joan and I had, something that she'd never experienced with Gerald. She either wanted to replace Joan or she wanted to replace me in our relationship, and I was certain her preference was one that would exclude myself. With this thought the imaginary plan to murder Olivia faded; I realised that irrespective of whether I killed her or not, I was at risk of losing Joan, either because she couldn't forgive me for murdering her new friend, or through Olivia's manipulative persuasion a wedge would be driven between Joan and I.

I was suddenly aware that Joan had woken up and was looking at me.

"You were deep in thought, what were you thinking about?" she asked with a smile and leant across and kissed me on the cheek.

"I don't think Olivia likes me." I announced, Joan was about to interrupt and protest, but I continued quickly before she had a chance. "You've seen for yourself how she ignores most of what I say and only responds by talking to you as if I wasn't there. I certainly don't think she trusts me. I've also been thinking about different explanations for why Gerald would just leave Olivia and disappear, but I need you to talk with her first to find out some details of who she is and her financial circumstances." I realised I'd started gabbling so I thought it better not to say anymore.

"I think we need to get up, go downstairs and sit with a cup of coffee and you can tell me your thoughts, I sense you've been awake half the night thinking about all of these things." I gave her a twisted smile and nodded as we climbed out of bed and went downstairs where I slumped into a chair at the table while Joan made some coffee and toast. I pulled over the note pad and pen and began to write out the information I needed Joan to wheedle out of Olivia and with a brief explanation of why:-

    1) What happens after we've buried Gerald if Olivia doesn't do anything, like reporting him missing to the police. Who would notice he was missing and after how much time would it be before they noticed:-

    • Does he have any family? Does he have any friends? Mistresses?

    • Did Gerald work? Would colleagues notice?

- Does Gerald have life insurances? Would Olivia have financial difficulties if Gerald simply went missing? A large life insurance policy could be considered a motive for a murder.
- Did Gerald have any secret, quiet places that he went to, perhaps for a walk or just to sit quietly in the car reading a paper or for any other reason? Trying to think of a secluded but likely place he would go by himself where we could abandon his car.

Joan sat down with the coffees and toast and immediately continued our conversation. "I agree with why you think Olivia doesn't like you, I think I need to have a conversation with her to find out if it's just you or if it's all men. I told you she'd been having a difficult time with Gerald; she even told us she was relieved he was dead. I'm certain it's not you personally, although I know you can be a bit of an irritating twat at times!" We both laughed, lightening my feelings of anxiety. "Ok, tell me what you want me to ask Olivia and why."

CHAPTER 17.

MANY THINGS CHANGED for us over the next few months. My feelings of irritation and anxiety with the intrusion of Olivia into our lives grew daily. I thought her objectives were obvious, particularly when I heard her speak softly, kindly and persuasively to Joan, constantly offering warm and tender affection that I felt was excessive and on occasions, obsessive . But Joan seemed blind to the manipulative control that Olivia had begun to exercise over her, as she also seemed blind to Olivia's attitude and the way she spoke to me, which had now become even more abrupt and rude.

Often their intimacy left me feeling isolated as they spent increasing amounts of time together; they went out for lunch or dinner at least a couple of times a week and occasionally away for a short weekend break. Very rarely was I ever invited. The fun and joy, the close companionship and the deep love that had bonded Joan and I together for the decades of our marriage, had very much been eroded. On occasions Joan had even begun to treat me in a similar manner to the way Olivia treated me.

As they progressively became inseparable friends my feelings of anxiety changed to one of growing anger, jealousy and paranoia. I increasingly sat brooding on the situation, alone at the kitchen table, watching the evening sun turn to a darkness that seemed to match my mood while I reflected on how my current situation had evolved from that night of farce when we went out to bury Gerald.

※※※

Joan and I had arrived outside of Jaqueline, Olivia's friends house at 7.30, as agreed and parked our car just a little bit down the road so we could watch to see when Olivia left to go out for dinner. It was a dry September evening and dusk had now obscured the colours of early autumn as we waited. It was only 10 minutes before we saw her car pull out of the house and drive past us as they left; we had agreed that if she had turned and driven away from us it would indicate that there was a problem and we should leave. As all seemed to be well, I drove the car into Jaqueline's drive and again parked at the side close to the gate. Armed with my can of oil I made my first job to ease the hinges so it didn't make such a noise as it opened, which would be of particular importance when we returned later in the night to bury Gerald.

We unloaded our tools into the wheelbarrow, entered the garden through the now silent gate and walked down the path in the semi darkness, through the opening in the hedge and into the vegetable garden. We marked out the proposed edges of the grave, spread out a plastic sheet to one side where we could place the excavated soil and began to dig, taking great care to put the dark topsoil to one side for when we needed it later to disguise our excavations. I hadn't dug down a further 6 inches into the sandy/clay subsoil, before I was gasping for breath and the sweat was dripping from my brow. I'd never dug a grave before and hadn't realised how much materials came out of a hole that was six feet long by two feet wide. I stepped aside and handed the spade to Joan; we had agreed we would do this together and she'd insisted on taking her turn, something I could see she immediately regretted as she ineffectually did her best to scrape out little amounts of soil at a time; unfortunately most of this fell back in as she tried to throw it onto the ever growing pile at the side.

After an hour we had only managed to dig down about two feet and were both weary, Joan suggested that we take a break and incredibly produced a flask of coffee and poured out two cups before rummaging in her pocket and surprising me further by removing two chocolate Kit Kat's. The surprises weren't finished however, for when I took a sip of coffee I discovered it was heavily laced with brandy. 'What a woman' I thought as I smiled appreciatively at her.

Feeling suitably refreshed I began to dig with greater vigor and determination and as the soil became more sandy and lighter, the hole was soon just under five feet deep. Unfortunately, it became apparent that at this depth it was almost impossible for us to lift the shovels of earth over the edge of the hole and onto the plastic. It had also begun to get quite wet at the bottom of the hole and I had visions that if we tried to dig much deeper it would just become a mud bath and the sides may begin to collapse.

We stood looking down at the results of our efforts and decided it would just have to be deep enough. We wondered if smells would be able to escape from this shallower grave; we had read on the internet that it should be six feet deep, this was also to prevent animals digging the body back up. In the end we agreed this was the best we could do, it would just have to be sufficient, particularly as we were expecting a call quite soon from Olivia to tell us they were leaving the restaurant and we should leave so we wouldn't be seen. We spread another piece of plastic over the grave to protect it from any rain, left our tools alongside before retracing our steps back up the garden pushing the wheelbarrow, which we left beside the gate for later. We then carefully changed into clean shoes and put our muddy boots into bin bags. The phone suddenly rang three times before it stopped, which was Olivia's signal that they were on their way. We quickly finished cleaning ourselves with some old cloths, got into the car and drove back to Olivia's house to wait for her to return. The waiting was made much easier as we finished off Joan's very special coffee and it wasn't too long before she pulled her car into the drive and parked beside us, and we all got out.

"Sorry about the delay," apologised Olivia, "Jaqueline insisted I had a coffee with her when I went to drop her off, and then she wouldn't stop talking. The good thing is she's had a few drinks and claimed she was going straight to bed as soon as I left, so with a bit of luck we won't need to leave it too long before we go back and bury Gerald. How did you get on digging the grave?" She asked, opening her front door and we all walked in.

"It's not as deep as we wanted because we started to hit water and it was getting quite muddy, but I think it'll be OK." I replied.

"Do you think it'll be OK Joan?" She asked, almost as if my advice or opinion wasn't good enough; Olivia really annoyed me when she constantly doubted the things I said or ignored any suggestions I made. I couldn't understand what it was about me she didn't like or trust, and why she always felt the need to look to Joan for confirmation. I was tired and this latest blatant demand for an endorsement from Joan that the grave would be OK. I was angry and stepped forward, about to ask Olivia why she questioned everything I said, but Joan, anticipating my intentions, took my arm and replied.

"Brian's absolutely right, it was the best we could do, and I completely agree that it will be fine. The thing that has worried me more than the depth is Gerald's current bent, sitting posture, do you think we can straighten him out, so he'll lie flat and fit in the grave? How long does rigor mortis keep the body rigid, do you know?" She asked, looking questioningly at Olivia as we sat down at the kitchen table, avoiding all the unpleasant memories that going into the sitting room for more comfortable seats would've generated.

"That's a very good question Joan, I have no idea, but I'm sure it only lasts a short while after death, he certainly wouldn't fit in the grave in the position he was last night. Let me find out." She turned to face the kitchen counter and asked. "Alexa, how long does rigor mortis keep a human body rigid?"

"Here is what I've found." Replied a gentle, female, mechanical voice. "Rigor mortis is the stiffening of the joints in a human body that start between 1 and 3 hours after death has occurred and can take up to 72 hours for the tissues of the joints to decay and allow the release of the effects of rigor mortis. Did this answer your question?"

"72 hours," exclaimed Olivia, "I can't leave him in the boot of the car for another two days. Alexa," she demanded of the little black tube resting next to the kettle, "How do you straighten rigor mortis limbs?"

"I've found this on the web." Replied the passionless voice. "In the embalming process, embalmers first position the body. They then relieve rigor mortis by flexing, bending, and massaging the arms, legs and torso. They then move the limbs to a suitable position, usually with legs extended and arms at the sides or hanging over the edge of the table, so that blood can drain into and expand the vessels for better embalming. Does this answer your question?" We sat quietly contemplating this advice before Olivia broke the silence.

"This is just a nightmare. Does this mean we have to give Gerald a full body massage and a set of bending exercises to get him to lay flat so we can get him to fit in the grave?" Questioned Olivia, her voice trembling at the thought of having to perform such a treatment on her dead husband.

"The only other option would be to leave him in the boot of the car for another couple of days." I tried to sound positive.

"No," replied Olivia, "it's not right to leave Gerald stuffed in the boot of his car any longer than he already has been. He wasn't a particularly nice person of recent years, but nobody deserves that kind of indignity. We must bury him tonight and I think if we leave in about an hour, Jaqueline will be sound asleep, and we'll be finished in no time." She concluded with a look of determination. I wish I felt as positive as she did, and I could tell Joan had serious reservation about how easy Gerald's burial was going to be.

CHAPTER 18.

OLIVIA DROVE GERALD'S CAR with Joan sitting in the front and me relegated to my usual position in the back. When we first got in the car there was an unmistakable smell of unpleasantness that couldn't be easily described or identified as being like anything in particular. It was a smell that carried sweet and sour notes with some underlying farmyard elements, all blended together to form a thick, cloying atmosphere that made you grimace and put your hand over your face in a futile effort to prevent it leaving a permanent impression. I realised Olivia was right, we couldn't have left Gerald in the car any longer, certainly not for another two days, we would never have been able to get in the car never mind drive the mile or so to Jaqueline's house, even tonight was still very difficult and I was amazed none of us were sick.

Our plan was simple. We would drive to Jaqueline's house, silently we would lift Gerald out from the boot of the car, lay him in the wheelbarrow, push him down the garden, watch Olivia give him a massage, put him in the grave, backfill it with soil, tidy up, return to the car and drive back to Olivia's. Simple, what could possibly go wrong.

We drove over and parked once again in Jaqueline's drive; this time Olivia reversed back so the boot was close to the gate. We got out of the car, each of us wearing a pair of yellow marigold rubber gloves as if we were about to wash the dishes, and stood silently for a few minutes waiting to see if we'd attracted any attention, but all was still. We moved to the rear of the car and Olivia opened the boot; we all quickly stood back as the lid sprung open to reveal Gerald still resting on his side in a rigid sitting position, his left foot and head tucked under the edges of the boot. I don't think any of us really wanted to touch him never mind taking a firm hold to remove him from the car, but it was Joan who broke our inertia by whispering.

"We've got to do this Brian, if you take his shoulders, Olivia you lift him by his legs, and I'll lift his arms." We all moved into our designated positions and took hold of the cold, rigid corpse and when Joan told us to lift, we all groaned a little with our efforts. As we lifted, pulled and twisted, we finally managed to get one of his feet out over the edge of the boot before the rest of his body became stuck; his head remained wedged at one end and his other foot stuck at the other. We were all breathing heavily with the effort as we stood back to consider what we could do next.

"I think you're going to have to give him a back, neck and shoulder massage to get him loosened up Olivia." I suggested. She just glowered back at me accusingly as if this current situation was all my fault, but she knew I was right. I suppose I shouldn't have been relishing the thought of watching her perform this unfortunate, but necessary act on her husband. I did however manage throughout the entire process to maintain a facial expression that spoke of concern and sympathy, but my mind enjoyed every moment watching Olivia position herself half in and half out of the boot as she tried to massage Gerald's neck.

"Do you want me to try and waggle his head while your massaging." I asked helpfully.

"I'll do that," offered Joan when she saw the angry look that crossed Olivia's face.

After about 10 minutes Gerald's head and neck became limp and as Olivia moved to a new position that would allow her to rub Gerald's back, to my disappointment, Joan stopped her and suggested that we may be able to get him out without any further treatment; a suggestion that proved to be true as we again lifted, twisted and pulled, until with a sudden release Gerald's second foot came free and with me still pushing and lifting his body weight, it caused him to tumble over the back edge of the boot. I could do nothing to help except watch as the two girls tried to steady his rapid exodus but failing, causing Olivia to stumble backwards and collide with the wheelbarrow, which fell over making a loud scraping bang. Gerald then fell onto the drive with a loud thump and a crack that indicated something had broken. Fortunately, Gerald hadn't seemed to notice and we could see when Joan shone her torch that he was lying on his side, his head lolling at an odd angle; his facial expression hadn't changed and he obviously hadn't felt any pain, unlike Olivia who was sitting beside the fallen barrow rubbing her leg.

There wasn't any time to try and continue with our original plan which was to sit Gerald in the wheelbarrow and push him through the gate and down the garden path, as an upstairs light had come on and a face appeared at the window, it was Jaqueline. It was at this moment that Olivia went right up in my esteem as she quickly leapt up and ran into the light that shone down from the window above and started waving her hands. The window opened and Jaqueline's head appeared.

"Olivia, what's wrong, are you alright?"

"Jaqueline, I'm really sorry to disturb you but I left my purse in your kitchen, it's got my phone and everything in it and I need it urgently, can you let me in for a minute so I can get it and then I'll let you go back to sleep." Explained Olivia most convincingly.

"I'll come straight down and let you in." Agreed Jacqueline as she shut the window.

Olivia ran back over and quickly helped Joan and I drag Gerald through the gate into the darkness of the garden, I then ran back to get the wheelbarrow while Olivia composed herself at Jaqueline's front door. Joan and I stood quietly listening as we heard the door open and muffled voices talking before the door shut and we were left in the darkness with Gerald at our feet and me still holding the wheelbarrow. Our hearts were racing as I whispered to Joan.

"Do you think this night could get any worse?" She didn't get a chance to reply as we heard the front door reopen and further muffled voices followed by the sound of Olivia starting up the car and driving out of the drive, away down the road and into the distance. Complete silence returned while we continued to remain still. As the minutes ticked by, I finally whispered to Joan.

"Do you think she's just fucked off and left us?"

"Don't be daft Brian, she's not going to leave us to it, she'll be hiding out at the front watching and waiting for Jaqueline to settle back to sleep." Joan sounded confident. The minutes continued to tick by and after several more had passed, Joan whispered again.

"She'll not be much longer." This time her voice didn't sound so confident. "We could try and get Gerald into the wheelbarrow and start pushing him down the garden, I feel a bit worried that we're hiding so close to the house. If you lean him forward so he's balancing on his toes, I'll push the barrow behind and we can lower him into it. What do you think?" I couldn't think of anything else we could do so we both levered Gerald upright and I held him in this position as Joan pushed the wheelbarrow so it went behind his knees and I carefully lowered him backward as Joan continued to brace the barrow. Remarkably as Gerald's buttocks arrived in the centre of the barrow and Joan continuing to hold it steady, everything seemed to balance. Gerald just sat there, his hands on his knees, his legs bent over the front and his head, although tilted a little un-naturally to the side, his face was still facing to the front as if he was looking forward to the wheelbarrow ride down the garden. We tried not to disappoint him as we set off, with an unstable wobble, down the path.

We had only gone about twenty yards when a voice whispered from behind giving us both a fright and nearly causing the wheelbarrow to go off course and into the box hedging that bordered the path.

"I think she's gone to sleep; all the lights are off. How are you managing?" Asked Olivia.

"We're getting there slowly." I replied, I had a suspicion that Olivia had been watching us for some time and knew exactly how the two of us were struggling. "You could help Joan balance Gerald to stop him falling over and if you shine a torch on the path ahead it would help me see where I'm going which will speed things up."

It was much easier with the three of us and very quickly we arrived in the vegetable garden, where we lifted Gerald out of the wheelbarrow and laid him face up on the ground, his legs pointing up in the air and his knees bent. We all stood looking down at him, we knew what needed to be done, and I suspected we all knew who had to do it.

"Olivia, you're going to have to massage his thighs and knees to straighten his legs." In the light of our torches I saw her glare at me, I knew it wasn't because of what I'd said but I think she knew the pleasure I was getting from her discomfort. "I'll start taking off the plastic sheeting and check the grave." I gave her a final smile.

Olivia got to work massaging Gerald's upper thighs, I'm sure in the dim reflective light I could see a smile appear on his face as his head rolled casually from side to side to the rhythm of the hands that were vigorously rubbing. Olivia had recruited Joan to help and she was kneeling beside Olivia massaging the left knee and flexing the leg in an effort to straighten it. Surprisingly, within minutes they had succeeded and moved on to work on his other side. By the time I had everything in and around the grave prepared, Gerald was lying perfectly flat on the ground.

It was a simple process to lift the body and drop him, quite unceremoniously, into the grave where he landed with a small splash at the bottom; it was a perfect fit. Olivia and Joan stood side by side, I could tell they were saying goodbye and giving apologies respectively, I was just thrilled that he was finally lying in the hole and I immediately started shoveling: first the sandy/clay soil, carefully pushing it around the body and compacting it as thoroughly as possible. Finally, I shoveled the black topsoil over and carefully raked the entire area, before spreading some leaves and other detritus around to complete and conceal what lay beneath. We quickly collected the tools, the plastic sheeting and after carefully checking that all looked relatively undisturbed, we walked back up the garden, through the gate, across the drive, onto the road where we walked about 200 yards to where Olivia had parked the car. After we'd wrapped everything, changed our shoes, cleaned ourselves up and driven back to Olivia's house it was 1.30 in the morning and for all we were very tired we still had several things to do.

The first was to remove everything from Gerald's car, including the plastic protective sheet we'd put in the boot to lay Gerald on. The car then needed to be thoroughly wiped down, particularly where his head and foot had been wedged. With everything ready, I then drove Gerald's car while following Olivia who drove her own, Joan had decided to accompany

Olivia, 'to give her some support during this stressful time', was her verbal reasoning, but I knew she was going to seek answers to our questions.

We drove for almost an hour, well into the countryside before Olivia drove down a narrow little lane that eventually arrived at a small car park in front of a lake that had a sign attached to it that read – *PRIVATE FISHING by prior arrangement only.* She parked the car over in a corner. Joan walked over and got into the passenger seat while I climbed into the back seat to allow Olivia to drive her car; I saw she took a small detour to place Gerald's car keys in the grass close to the water's edge, so it would look as if they'd been dropped. She then got into the car and drove us quietly away. It had started raining as we reached the main road, a damp soaking rain that seemed to reflect the sombre occasion.

We drove silently back to Olivia's house, there wasn't anything left to talk about, or rather I sensed there was nothing to talk about in my presence, I suspected that Joan and Olivia would have had plenty to talk about if I wasn't there. We collected our car, it was now raining heavily, and drove home, completely exhausted; we both agreed that although there was much for us to discuss, we would leave it until the morning after we'd had some sleep.

CHAPTER 19.

IT FELT GREAT TO FEEL a degree of 'normality' returning to our lives as Joan and I sat once again at the kitchen table, it had been a maniacal couple of days; they had been so long and stressful they'd felt like a week. Several times during the night I'd woken up and rerun the images from the night before, viewing them like a low grade, ridiculous black and white Laurel and Hardy movie; unfortunately in the cold light of the morning I realised that these images were probably a true reflection of how we all must have looked in the garden of Jaqueline's.

Joan had cooked some scrambled eggs on toast, which we'd just finished and had sat back to drink our coffee.

"I managed to find out lots of things about Olivia when we drove to the fishing lake, she's such a lovely person and I know she and I are going to be great friends," announced Joan. "I wish you'd stop irritating her so much, you always seem so aggressive when you speak to her, why do you do that, it makes me feel uncomfortable, never mind her?"

"I don't know what it is about her, but I don't particularly like or trust her and I get the feeling she feels the same about me. She seems to bring out the worst in me, but for your sake I'll try harder in the future, hopefully we won't have to see her again."

"Well, I intend to see her quite regularly and I'm actually meeting up with her for lunch tomorrow in town, but I wasn't going to invite you knowing how you feel about her."

"Just be careful," I advised. "So, what did you learn about her?"

"You wanted to know who would miss Gerald if Olivia didn't report him as missing or do anything more. According to her, absolutely nobody would. The only relative he has is a brother who he hasn't spoken to for years and Olivia has never even met. She herself was an only child and met Gerald about five years ago through a dating agency after she'd been single for many years following a divorce from her first husband, who has since died.

When I asked if Gerald had any friends or work colleagues who would miss him, she just laughed and explained that he'd never worked for years and lived off her money entirely. He'd become an idle, kept man. She'd discovered shortly after they were married, that he had absolutely nothing and was quite deep in debt. He really enjoyed the high life, which was one of the traits which had convinced her at the time that he was a man of substance; he'd also been fun loving and very charismatic and romantic with her, until after they were married. He had several acquaintances that he met when he occasionally played golf or went fishing, but no friends, nobody would miss him she'd told me.

It was when I asked her if Gerald had any life insurances or valuable assets that she became quite angry, not at me but at the thought that anyone could consider she may have killed him for his money. She told me that it was her that had all the money, assets and property when they got married; she'd inherited a fortune from her parents when they died and had also received a substantial sum when she divorced her first 'cheating bastard' of a husband. It was her divorce lawyer who advised her to complete a Prenuptial Agreement if she were ever to re-marry, fortunately for her she did, otherwise apparently Gerald would've spent the lot. It was this situation that had caused the conflict in their marriage, and he had over the past couple of years started shouting and hurting her whenever the topic of money came up. He was always demanding more and more and was trying to make her cancel the agreement, but she'd refused and kept their finances completely separate and remained very strict about controlling the amount he had available to spend; she said she gave him a substantial allowance, which sounded a bit 'Victorian', but I suspect she knew what she was doing. She told me again how pleased she was to be rid of him. I think after what she told me it also explains why she doesn't have a high opinion of men."

"Did you tell her that she could trust me." I asked.

"What, get her to trust the man who lost our entire wealth and has driven me to a life of crime," she laughed, "I'm not that persuasive!" I threw my napkin at her and laughed also, but I did wonder how much of our recent situation Joan had confided to Olivia, and had Olivia used her own recent marital experiences to highlight the failings of all men, in particular my own culpability in the loss of our pensions and savings. I suddenly felt a little paranoid and anxious at the prospect of their growing friendship; why would Olivia want a friendship with

Joan, someone who only two nights ago was robbing her of her money? Joan began clearing the table and I got up to help, I realised that my thoughts had caused me to drift away a bit and I hadn't commented on all the information Joan had discovered.

"Sorry Joan, I got distracted for a moment, you told me so much information I was trying to work out how it affected what we should suggest Olivia does next and how we can help her." I explained.

"Olivia and I did talk about this and your suggested options, the one where she does nothing and simply waits until someone comes to ask after Gerald or why his car was permanently parked at the fishing lake, is her preference. She's just going to pretend that he walked out on her after he'd demanded she get a load of cash out of the bank and she's never seen or heard from him since. She's going to plead complete ignorance of his whereabouts and only report him missing if she's asked to. I don't think there's anything we can do except support her by being good friends, and who knows, one day she may realise what a lovely man you are." She smiled and kissed me on the forehead before starting to wash our breakfast dishes. I didn't feel reassured, I felt left out.

CHAPTER 20.

THE NEXT EVENT that caused me even greater concern was when I became certain that Joan and Olivia had gone into 'partnership' together.

Joan and I had agreed that our life of crime ought to be paused for a while, the events surrounding the death of Gerald had left a lasting impression and reduced our enthusiasm for further ventures. We had done very well over the past few months and accrued enough money to keep us going for quite a while.

This is what I thought we'd agreed, but I soon discovered that it was not entirely correct, apparently it was me who thought we should pause our life of crime, and it was me who had lost my enthusiasm for further ventures. Not Joan.

I knew Joan and Olivia had become very close friends and they went out together quite often, I believed it was to enjoy lunches, dinners and the occasional overnight shopping trip away in the city; she even told me about the things she'd nearly bought and the shows and films she'd been to see. But she was lying.

It was the little things I noticed at first. I was never invited to any of these little outings, Joan explained this by pointing out the obvious; Olivia and I irritated each other. Joan never seemed to return from any of these trips with anything new; no new clothes, shoes, make up or even a magazine. She never seemed to spend anything, I constantly suggested she take some money, but she told me that Olivia knew our circumstances and insisted on paying for everything. Joan was always picked up by Olivia, even when I offered to drop her off.

I then began to notice some quite odd things; I'd been looking for my gloves and noticed our balaclavas were missing, initially I just assumed they were being washed, but later I returned to our bedroom and checked Joan's wardrobe and draws but couldn't find any of her 'criminal' clothes either; again I assumed logically that they were probably being washed along with the balaclavas. After Joan returned from her 'trip' I checked the bedroom again to discover all these 'missing' things were now in their rightful place and when I smelt the balaclavas, Joan's smelt of Joan and mine now smelt of a perfume, which I immediately suspected was Olivia's.

As the days and weeks passed, I watched closely to see if I could discover what was happening; I listened through the closed door when Olivia came over 'for a chat', I listened in as best as I could to every phone call and watched most carefully and regularly to see if and when the balaclavas were removed from the draw. I was nearly caught a few times in different situations, and I did wonder if Joan was suspicious that I suspected she was planning another heist.

During these increasingly frequent times when I was alone, I would often spend long periods talking to my friend:-

"I don't know what they're up to, do you have any idea?" I'd ask.

"She's away out again with the evil Madam Olivia Armstrong - gone to do some shopping she said, and have some lunch apparently, won't be back until later. You'd think people would be surprised when they turned up to these social events dressed in black and wearing balaclavas! I don't believe a word she says, does she tell you the same?"

"I'm going to cook a gammon steak with chips and a fried egg for my tea, would you like to join me?"

My questions were never answered, and I rarely received any recognition that I was even talking to him, unless of course I said a sentence with the word 'Walk' in it, then Wolfie immediately became very attentive. He was very cute and was always there, and he may have starred in many children's stories, but he couldn't cook, couldn't clean, couldn't iron; I'd even had to start cutting the grass and tending the garden myself! His company really wasn't a replacement for Joan.

Another concerning and inexplicable thing began to happen, I started feeling unwell. At first, I only felt a little nauseous, particularly after I'd eaten, and I simply explained this away by convincing myself that I'd eaten too much, or the food had been too rich or fatty. But then to accompany this nauseous feeling, I began to get a pain in my chest; it wasn't really in my chest but emanated from the general area of my solar plexus. I didn't believe it was bad enough to ask the doctor, so I did what all sensible people do and checked on the internet to make a 'self-diagnosis', and of course the explanation given was obvious as I read:-

'Anxiety is a common cause of **solar plexus pain***. The* **solar plexus** *is tied to the adrenal glands and the lungs. The fight-or-flight response to stress can result in poor breathing. This can lead to* **pain** *or other gastric symptoms like nausea or vomiting during episodes of anxiety.'*

"Phew!" I whispered to myself, "that's a relief, I thought I was having a heart attack!"

I concentrated on relaxing and even bought some herbal remedies to relive my 'stress', but no matter what I tried the symptoms became worse, the pain in my chest was sometimes quite severe. I suddenly thought of Gerald, had he had any symptoms like mine? Was I now the victim of poisoning? Once this thought had crept into my mind it wouldn't go away, particularly as I realised that if I were being poisoned it could only be by Joan's hand, presumably being guided by the evil Olivia.

I changed tactics. Whenever Joan cooked and served a meal or poured me a drink, I left it, usually explaining that I wasn't hungry or thirsty, and whenever I could I threw it away and pretended I'd eaten or drank it. I purchased my own food and drink, which I kept down in the garden shed and secretly ate and drank whenever I claimed to need a tool or do some gardening; activities had become much more regular to justify these trips to the bottom of the garden. But despite all my careful efforts, nothing improved, and my symptoms continued to worsen. How were they doing this? Was there some sort of cream that Joan was managing to put on my skin? Was the poison in my shampoo? Was there something that was being sprayed on my clothes or my pillow? All these thoughts went through my mind, I realised I couldn't escape unless I actually packed a bag and left Joan, but I worried if I did that it would mean the evil bitch Olivia would've won, and how long would it be before she tired of Joan and began to poison her?

My level of anxiety reached new heights when Joan told me that she and Olivia were having a night away at a Spa Hotel out in the country the following weekend. She promised to leave me all my favorite treats so I wouldn't starve, and gave me what I felt was a rather dismissive kiss on the cheek; it hadn't been that long ago it would've been not just a quick kiss but a loving hug as well; it wasn't that long ago she wouldn't have been going away without me at all! I decided that with this current situation, and for the sake of our relationship and to save our marriage, it was time for me to become more proactive and end the pervasive control that Olivia had over my beloved Joan. When I saw that our balaclavas and Joan's 'criminal' outfit were no longer where they should be, I decided to follow them to this 'imaginary' Spa Hotel.

CHAPTER 21.

ALTHOUGH TIME WAS SHORT, I quickly managed to hire a car and stock it with things to eat, drink and to keep me warm and as comfortable as possible. I also loaded much of our 'Private Investigator's' equipment; binoculars, camera, and just in case, my 'gentrified landscape gardener' disguise; I smiled as I promised myself not to speak like a pirate as Joan had accused me of doing all those months ago.

Joan said Olivia was picking her up at 10.00am and ten minutes before she was due to arrive I told Joan I was going for a walk and we said our goodbyes; I think she believed I didn't want to be around when Olivia arrived, which was true to an extent, but obviously my real intention was to walk around to an adjacent street where I'd parked the hire car and drive to the end where I could observe Olivia's arrival and then easily pull in behind them when they left so I could observe where they went and what they did.

I didn't have to wait very long and as Olivia pulled up outside our house, I could see Joan locking up and walking to the car with her small suitcase. I followed at a respectable distance and was surprised that they only drove the few miles across town to Olivia house where they parked, got out and went into the house with Joan carrying her suitcase. I parked some distance up a side road that gave me a clear view of the house and waited, expecting them to return to the car quite soon so they may commence their journey.

I sat there for eleven and a half hours. Eleven and a half fucking hours. It had become pitch black dark, I'd eaten all my food, finished all my drinks and filled all the empty bottles with urine; I'd had no other choice, and since the bottle tops were not particularly large and I'd never had much experience of pissing into one, (particularly in the cramped confines of a car whilst trying to be as discreet as possible since I was on a public street with houses on both sides), there had been one or two accidents that fortunately had now dried up, but had left me feeling a little uncomfortable. One of the scientific observations I had discovered from this experience was how the laws of physics appear to be constantly broken; how was it there always seemed to be twice as much liquid came out from what went in. Not only had I filled the empty water bottles, but I'd had to empty another bottle of water before using that, and incredibly I'd also had to use my flask; I vowed I'd never drink tea out of it again. Eleven and a half fucking hours – what sort of moron sat spying on his wife, pissing in his tea flask and feeling miserable for that long!

Several times I felt like giving up. I was starting to believe that Joan and Olivia weren't going out at all and were perhaps just having an innocent 'girls' night in watching movies and I had just become a paranoid, foolish old man who was now suffering with serious chest pains, feeling sick and also chronic heartburn; a new condition that had been added to the list of my symptoms. I was just thinking I should probably drive to the nearest A & E rather than going straight home, when suddenly the outside lights of Olivia's house came on and the two women walked out, all dressed in black; through the binoculars I could see that Joan had her 'criminal' outfit on. The car quickly reversed and turned to drive back out onto the road; I quickly drove to the end of the side road and turned right to follow them.

They were easy to follow; Olivia was not a fast driver and I managed to maintain a safe distance behind the car without losing them. We drove out of town and after about a mile they turned onto a minor road that led to a village perched on a steep hill. They parked just up from the village store, opposite a driveway that I could see had pillars either side with pretentious carved lion statues perched on top. Joan and Olivia both got out of the car, walked to the rear and took out of the boot a cardboard box; from the look of it I was certain it was the same box Joan and I had used when we went to rob Olivia and Gerald. I was a little disappointed they hadn't been more creative and come up with a new sort of robbery.

As they walked through the entrance to the drive, I couldn't see them as it was dark, and my sight was largely obscured by the fence and shrubbery. I waited a few minutes before my curiosity got the better of me and decided to drive past the gate and park the car further down the hill and walk back up so I could see what was going on. I'd just started the car and was about to drive forward when Joan came running out of the gate and started sprinting down the hill away from the house; I'd never seen Joan move so fast in my life, sprinting wasn't really a true description of her movement, more like a brisk hobble with a hint of jogging. However, I instantly realised she was in trouble and accelerated quickly to catch up and get her into the car to aid her escape. As

I accelerated and approached the gate I had to swerve in an effort to avoid hitting Olivia who sprinted out into the road, obviously with the intention of getting to her car, but I knew it was too late; I closed my eyes and heard the tyres screech followed by a crunching, sickening impact before completely losing control as the front wheel bounced over the body I'd collided with. The car continued to skid and finally came to a loud crashing halt as it hit the gate pillar. My head and body were instantly consumed by the airbag which brutally wrapped itself around my head, neck and shoulders, knocking the wind and consciousness out of me.

I briefly came around a short time later with an elderly man standing in the now open door of the car.

"Stay still," he instructed, "my wife has called an ambulance and it's on it's way." I couldn't reply, I couldn't get my breath and the pain in my chest had become all-consuming and now expanded to my shoulder, upper back and neck. 'This is it' I thought, 'I'm dying.' I then must have passed out because the next thing I knew I was being lifted into the back of an ambulance. I could see quite a few blue flashing lights and a policeman wearing an overall that stated POLICE ARMED RESPONSE UNIT, he stood close to the back of the ambulance talking to the old man. I hoped Joan hadn't been shot was the last thing I remember thinking until I came around in the intensive care unit with a nurse speaking loudly at me as she instructed.

"Mr. Collins, BREATHE."

I was confused, I couldn't entirely remember why I was here or what had happened, and lay quietly concentrating on trying to do as the nurse had instructed, but as she kept shouting at me I obviously wasn't doing it properly; I kept going back to sleep and forgetting. Fortunately, it wasn't too long before I awoke properly. I soon was able to speak and began to feel more coherent, finally managing to ask what had happened.

"You apparently had a car crash. You weren't badly injured but you were seriously unwell when you arrived here and you've had to undergo an emergency operation to remove your gall bladder, which was seriously infected and the ducts were completely blocked with stones. You must have felt unwell and in serious pain for quite a while and should've had treatment much sooner.!" The nurse explained.

"Have I not been poisoned, I thought someone had poisoned me?" I asked sounding a little hysterical. The nurse frowned questioningly.

"No, why would you think you'd been poisoned?" 'Fuck,' I thought, 'to explain that would take hours.' The explanation I gave was much simpler and acceptable.

"I think I'm just confused, probably with the anesthetic!" I then asked the question I really feared the answer to. "How's the person I knocked down?" I didn't want to tell anyone I knew it was a woman, and that I knew her well, and that she was the person I thought had been poisoning me! Again, the nurse's brow creased.

"I was only told that you'd hit a dog that ran out into the road in front of you, I haven't heard anything other than that. Your wife and her friend are in the waiting room, I'll tell them that I'll be taking you back down to the ward in about twenty minutes and they can see you then, if you're feeling up to having visitors. She'll be able to tell you more about your accident. The police were here earlier, and I know they spoke to her and want to speak with you when you feel up to it." It was my turn to frown questioningly, but with surprise as the nurse left.

Half an hour later Joan and Olivia walked up to my bedside, both smiled at me with concern until the nurse had stopped hovering and left us alone, then their smiles changed to faces full of questions.

"Brian, what the hell were you doing there?" Demanded Joan, taking my hand.

"Never mind that, what the hell are you two doing here? Why haven't you been arrested?" I demanded more forcibly, releasing Joan's hand, all wooziness now having disappeared. I tried to sit up so I could focus my attention better and they both helped by placing pillows behind my back as supports, I suspected their fussing was just a delaying tactic. I lay with my arms over my chest and the gown that covered the bandages and stared at them, waiting for an answer.

"This is all my fault," admitted Olivia, "and the only way I can explain is to tell you the truth from the beginning. I think Joan will have told you about my relationship with Gerald and the difficulties we had over the past couple of years, but what she hasn't told you, because I asked her not to, was that I have cancer and the prognosis is not good. My health caused further stress between Gerald and I; he was never particularly sympathetic or supportive during my diagnosis or treatment, his only true interest was his persistent attempts to gain control of my estate before my death so there would be no complications. I constantly refused and he became increasingly aggressive. You know I was relieved that he died, and you helped me avoid an extremely difficult situation if his death had been discovered. You'll be interested to hear that the police did come to the house to advise me that Gerald's car had been reported as possibly abandoned at the fishing lake. I invited them in and explained how he'd asked me to take some cash out of the bank and when I returned, he'd left. I told them we'd been arguing and his storming out was not unusual and he often stayed away for days, but as it had been about ten days since he 'left', and with the discovery of his car, I asked if they thought I should to report him missing. They suggested I call by the police station and fill out the paperwork and arrange for the car to be collected, which I did. That was over a month ago, and I haven't heard anything more from them; I could tell they weren't really interested and believed he'd just run away with a younger woman and I didn't do anything to dissuade them." Olivia was interrupted by the nurse who came back into the room to check if I was alright and if I wanted a hot drink or anything, I thanked her and said I was feeling fine and when she finished checking me over, she left.

Olivia continued her story. "The ironic thing was that, as I don't have any living relatives I had left the bulk of my money to Gerald anyway, if he'd just been a bit more pleasant and patient he would've been a wealthy man in the next few months." She paused, obviously upset at having vocalised the immanency of her own death. Joan started to come around the bed to comfort her, but Olivia waved her to stay where she was and continued.

"I wanted to have some excitement, something to stop me sitting at home dwelling on my deteriorating condition. I became so inspired by your audacious activities that Joan told me about as we got to know and confided in each other. She told me what you'd been doing and why you'd done them. I wanted to live yours and Joan's life in the time I had left, and I'm sorry if I wasn't pleasant to you Brian, I didn't want you preventing Joan from helping me; as you also may have guessed, I don't hold men in general with much regard. I'm sorry again for treating you badly, you didn't deserve that." She paused, a look of genuine regret on her face before she continued her explanation.

"Joan and I focused on the hostage/cash out of bank routine that you had done to Gerald and I; we'd already carried out one successful 'operation' and were carrying out the second when it all went wrong. We'd parked almost opposite the house." I nearly interrupted to say that I had followed them there and was watching but decided not to interrupt. "We walked up towards the house carrying the empty box, pausing behind some bushes to put on our balaclava's and get our toy guns out before walking up to the front door. We put the box down, rang the bell and stood to the side waiting for the door to be opened. An old man answered, and his attention immediately focused on the box, we jumped out, pointed our guns threateningly and pushed him back into the house. What happened next was a complete surprise since we'd carefully watched the house and all the comings and goings for a week and we'd never seen and therefore never expected to encounter a dog. As soon as we entered we realised the old man must've been preparing to go out as he was holding a lead with a large and extremely aggressive Alsatian dog attached to it. It started barking and snarling so Joan and I turned on our heals and ran. The dog, fortunately for us, struggled to chase us as he was held back by the old man who tried to hold onto his lead. We ran, I tripped and fell which let Joan escape out of the gate first, I quickly got up and began to run as fast as I could, particularly when I realised the old man had released the dog and it was already gaining on me rapidly. I ran out of the gate, intending to run straight across the road to my car, I never saw the oncoming car until the last minute and it swerved, missing me by inches but hit the dog before crashing into the gate pillar. I never looked back. I jumped into the car and set off driving down the street until I caught up with Joan and we drove home and got changed. We were just going to pour ourselves a drink when Joan's mobile phone rang, it was the police to tell her that a man had been injured in a car crash and his license and car hire documents identified him as you. They told us where you were, and we came straight over. The police were already here, they wanted to interview you as soon as you recovered sufficiently. They told us there'd been an attempted armed robbery and you'd been involved in a road accident as the criminals ran into the road to escape. When we asked where this had happened, they gave us details of the house in the village we'd been trying to rob and we immediately realised it had been you who'd been driving the car. I don't know what you were doing there Brian, and I'm sorry for causing you to crash the car and get injured, but if you hadn't arrived at that exact moment the dog would've caught me and I can't bear to think of the consequences. We cannot thank you enough and are so pleased you weren't seriously injured. I understand the biggest problem the medics faced was your serious chest pains; you kept telling them you'd been poisoned and were having a heart attack, but you were obviously confused. Thank you again Brian." Olivia leant over and kissed me on the cheek. I wanted to say something about her sad personal situation, but decided the moment wasn't right.

I waited for Joan to give me a similar embrace and thank me with the same level of gratitude that Olivia had shown, but as I turned to look at her I could see she wasn't being at all conciliatory, in fact she had her 'stern' face on.

"So, Brian, tell us what you were doing there, driving a strange car, late in the evening and past your bedtime?"

"I suspected what you were doing but wanted to know for certain. I didn't want you to know I was suspicious, and never expected you to find out I was following you. I hired a car so you wouldn't recognise it and when Olivia picked you up from our house this morning, I followed you back to her house. I sat and waited for over eleven hours before you left. I was so angry that you'd lied to me I was determined not to give up, even though I didn't feel very well. I followed you and watched you park the car, take out the box and go to the house, I was only moving the car so I could get a better view when you came running out. I realised you were in trouble and accelerated to catch you up and give you a lift. As I came to the gate a figure ran out in front of me, I thought it was Olivia and I was sure I'd hit her, I even felt the wheels going over her body." I shuddered at the memory. "There was then a loud crash and I don't really remember anything much after that. I do remember a policeman with a gun and a jacket that said ARMED POLICE UNIT, but that was only vaguely. I then woke up in the hospital and apparently all the chest, shoulder and back pains and the feelings of nausea were caused by gall stones and infection."

"So, you were spying on us?"

"Yes, and it's just as well or you'd be locked up by now and then who would I get to cook my dinner?" Joan finally smiled but before she could say any more, the nurse returned.

"The police are here to take your statement, are you feeling up to talking to them, I can tell them to come back later if you want?"

"No, I'll speak to them now, they'll want me to tell them everything I know." I said with a questioning smile at Joan that dared her to say another word. "Can my wife and her friend wait until they're finished, just in case the police need to speak to them for any reason?" Joan and Olivia left with a look of uncertainty which made me smile. They were replaced by a plain clothed officer who introduced himself as Detective Constable Wilkinson, who looked like a boy of about seventeen. He pulled up a seat and took out his notebook.

"How are you feeling Mr. Collins." The detective asked. "I hear you didn't suffer any serious injuries in the crash, but you had other underlying health issues that caused an emergency situation?"

"I don't remember too much about the crash. I know I wasn't going very fast and that I'd felt a little sick and had some stomach ache for an hour or two before the accident, but hadn't realised it would develop into anything serious. I am feeling so much better now, thank you."

"Can you tell me what you do remember?"

"Yes, I was driving along through a village, looking for somewhere to stop and have a drink before going home, when suddenly a figure ran out in front of me. I swerved, but nevertheless I thought I'd hit the person as there was a loud thump and then the front wheel of the car went over something, which I thought was the person I'd hit." I grimaced again at the memory. "The car then crashed into a wall, after which I don't remember much until I woke up a while ago here in hospital having had my gallbladder removed. Did I injure anyone? The nurse said I'd hit a dog, but I didn't see any dog.?"

"Well Mr. Collins, the nurse was right, you didn't hit anyone that we can establish, but you did hit a dog, which unfortunately seems to have been killed instantly." I gave a sad look before asking.

"Whose dog was it, I must apologise, it was an accident, but I will be quite willing to compensate the owners." I sounded sickeningly innocent.

"That's something you can contact them about yourself, but under the circumstances I think they'll probably wish to apologise to you as the gentleman owner has stated he lost control of the dog under an extreme circumstance. Can I ask you, this figure that ran out in front of you causing you to swerve, was it a man or a woman?" I pretended to think about this before replying.

"I'm sorry, I cannot be certain, it all happened so quickly, the figure came out onto the road so fast, the headlights flashed over them, they were definitely in black, in fact now I come to think about it the figure was all in black, including their head and face, I can't think exactly what they were wearing but they were definitely completely covered."

"Was the person carrying anything in their hands." Again, I paused before replying.

"I really couldn't be certain, but I don't think so, the person was just all in black and I swerved to avoid them; it all happened in a split second." The detective nodded, looking down at his notes, pausing before he asked.

"There's just one more thing Mr. Collins, and I don't think it has any relevance to the crash, but when we were removing your possessions from the car, we were a little confused to find several bottles and a flask of urine. Can you explain this?"

'Shit,' I thought, 'I'd forgotten about that.' "Oh'" I said, looking quite embarrassed, "Yes, you would've found that quite odd, but the answer is that I do some private detective work and I'd been on surveillance for a long time that evening, as you can gather, much longer than I anticipated. You'll find my business card in my wallet if you want to some details." I had impressed myself with this remarkably clever answer.

"Is that why you hired the car?"

"Yes, it is, I always do when I'm on that type of job, I don't want anyone recognising my own car, and I charge the cost back to the client."

"Can I ask where you'd been that evening and the name of your client?"

"I'm sorry," I replied, "that's confidential." The young detective looked at me as if I were impersonating 'Magnum'; I suspected if I mentioned the name of this famous P.I. to the young policeman he would wonder why I was thinking of impersonating an ice cream! "Is it relevant?" I asked.

"No, not really, it's just not something we often find at the scene of an accident. I think that's all my questions for time being Mr. Collins, I will take one of your business cards for our file and if I have any further questions I'll be in touch." He put an envelope on the side table, "I've left details of the initial report together with the incident number for the car hire company's insurance." I thanked him and he left. I was quickly rejoined by the two evil thieves themselves.

"What did he say?" asked Joan.

"What did you say?" asked Olivia.

"He just wanted to ask me what I'd witnessed, and to tell me that I'd killed a dog, and that they had a nationwide hunt out for two mature female thieves who'd attempted an armed robbery against an elderly, defenseless couple in their own home. He told me that the perpetrators of this dreadful crime had been caught on several CCTV cameras and he expected arrests would follow very soon. He also told me that in all his years of being a policeman he had never seen a robbery that had been so badly planned and executed so amateurishly; he couldn't wait to meet the two clowns involved." Olivia looked at me with terror. Joan stepped forward and gently cuffed the side of my head.

"You're such an arsehole Brian, he didn't know anything, did he?"

"Apart from me killing the dog, not a thing. He just wanted to give me a crime number and statement for the insurance" I confirmed, smiling back at her, then turning I noticed that tears had appeared in Olivia's eyes, I took her hand. "I'm sorry, I was only having a bit of fun, don't be upset, everything will be alright." I told her reassuringly.

"It's not alright for that poor dog, its death is all my fault." She wailed.

"We're all sorry about the dog. As I was the driver and am the only one who can legitimately go to the house and apologise, on behalf of us all, I will ask if there is anything I can do to ease their loss, like getting them a new dog, if you want." Olivia seemed satisfied with this suggestion and nodded her head gratefully.

Again, we were interrupted by the nurse, who told Olivia and Joan that they should go home and let me rest, she would call later in the day after the doctor had been around; she thought I would then probably be discharged and able to go home. I was soon left alone, I felt exceptionally well, better that I had done for sometime and I smiled at how foolish I'd been, imagine thinking I'd been poisoned, but as I began to sleep my smile disappeared as I thought of Olivia personal situation; I realised I was quite upset.

CHAPTER 22.

JOAN AND I STOOD in the chapel of the crematorium. I don't think either of us fully appreciated how few friends and family Olivia had. Apart from us there was only her friend Jaqueline, the owner of Gerald's grave, I only vaguely recognised her from that moment when she appeared at her bedroom window, on that difficult night, to investigate the noise in her drive. There was another elderly lady and a middle-aged man who Joan told me later were Olivia's housekeeper and gardener, she recognised them from her visits to Olivia's house. The only other person was a tall man who sat in the corner wearing a white shirt, a black tie and a dark suit, I thought he was probably one of the undertaker's entourage.

The service was simple and performed with dignity by the vicar of Olivia's local church, his words were quite generic as it was obvious he didn't really know Olivia, I think the last time he'd met her was when she married Gerald and he spoke confidently of that joyous day. Nobody mentioned Gerald or questioned why he wasn't here or where he was. It was reassuring that there was only two of us who knew the true answer.

During the service I held Joan's hand and I sensed throughout the service that she, like myself was reflecting over the past six months, a time during which Olivia, Joan and I had become inseparable friends. We'd spent virtually ever day together. We'd gone on many holidays together and enjoyed eating in some of the finest restaurants, we'd explored many of the most famous places and cities in Europe, we'd gone skiing in the Alps and cruised around the Caribbean. We had changed her life and she had changed ours, we couldn't have wished for a more fun loving, gentle, kind and generous friend. It was impossibly difficult to say goodbye, her condition deteriorated so suddenly, in the space of only a couple of weeks; there hadn't been enough time and we couldn't find the words or the heart to say goodbye properly. It was only now in the quietness of the chapel that we could let our feelings out as we both wept for the loss of our friend. Our lives would never be the same and we found it hard to imagine returning to our old life without her.

As we left the chapel we were approached by the tall man in the dark suit, he introduced himself as

Mr. Jefferson from Jefferson, Hardwick, Solicitors. He told us he represented Mrs. Armstrong and asked if we would attend his offices at a time convenient to ourselves, "Perhaps later this afternoon?" he'd suggested as he handed us his card. He explained there were some formal matters relating to Mrs. Armstrong's estate on which he needed to consult with us. We agreed a time of 4.00pm and he left, walking with a stooped grace that I decided made him look much more suited to be an undertaker than a solicitor

We were very curious at first, but as the hours moved closer to the time of our appointment, we had become a little worried. We had been speculating during lunch as to what the solicitor wanted to 'consult us' about, when I suddenly had a thought, a thought that made the blood drain from my face, as it did Joan's when I told her.

"What happened to Olivia's copy of the letter we all signed about our involvement in Gerald's death? Do you think Olivia left the letter with her solicitor to be opened if anything ever happened to her? We might be in trouble Joan." I concluded anxiously.

"Olivia wouldn't have done that, would she? If she did, she would've taken it back when we became such close friends, wouldn't she? Unless she forgot about it!" Joan had stopped eating her lunch and put down her knife and fork, her appetite crushed as a long-forgotten fear returned.

"We still have to go; things will only become even more difficult for us if we don't. I can't eat anything more, should we have a large brandy to give us some courage?" Joan nodded and I went to the bar thinking that the next couple of hours were going to feel like an eternity now we had nothing but our worries to occupy us while we waited for the appointment. As we sat sipping the drinks, our anxious silence seemed to spread throughout the bar as the lunchtime crowds left and we were almost the only customers left.

After another half hour we just couldn't sit still any longer and decided to slowly walk around the town, pretending to be interested in the shops, wishing we were at home playing with Wolfie in the garden. I thought he may be wondering where we were but wasn't certain if dogs had the mental capacity to fully understand time and be able to 'wonder' where anyone might be. I realised my thoughts were rambling and tried to focus on our uncertain future as we finally arrived at the offices of Jefferson, Hardwick, Solicitors.

The office was housed in a traditional, austere Victoria terraced block of well-maintained buildings close to the town centre. We opened the black painted door that held a highly polished brass plaque to confirm it was the offices of Jefferson, Hardwick, Solicitors. Expecting something that wouldn't have looked out of place in a Charles Dickens novel, we were surprised to be welcomed into a warm, tastefully modern reception area. We explained the arrangements we had with Mr. Jefferson to the receptionist and were shown to a comfortable, seated area where several other people were obviously waiting for their appointments.

I glanced around, trying to see if I could identify any of the room occupants as a plain clothed policeman and finally settled on one particular individual who seemed to take a great interest in all those present, particularly Joan and I; or so my feelings of paranoia would have me believe. People came and went, but my 'policeman' continued while he waited to watch everyone like a hawk. We were obviously very early, was he very early as well?

Finally, the receptionist arrived and asked if we would follow her. As we walked out, I noticed that the 'policeman' didn't follow; was he being left to prevent our escape if we decided to make a run for it? The relief that he hadn't followed us out, and the fact that everyone was so friendly, and that Mr. Jefferson especially stepped out of his office to greet us, lightened my dark feelings.

"Thank you for coming, can I offer you some tea?" He asked politely as he folded his large, angular frame into the chair behind his desk. I felt like shouting at him, 'No, just get on with it and put us out of our misery', but Joan replied before I could say anything.

"That would be very nice, tea for both of us, thank you." As I glanced across at her I could tell she sounded much more composed than she looked; Mr. Jefferson spoke into his phone to instruct his secretary to bring in some refreshments.

Turning to face us he spoke again with his calm, official voice. "As I mentioned as we left the Chapel of Rest, I represent Mrs. Olivia Armstrong and have done so for many years. It is a sad day that my final task on her behalf is as Executor of her affairs. I understand your relationship with her has not been of long standing, and when she last attended these offices she gave me explicit instructions on how to proceed in the event of her death." I swallowed hard as his tortuous explanation was suddenly brought to a halt with a knock on the door; I half expected the 'policeman' from the waiting room to walk in, but it was the secretary with a tray of china cups, matching milk jug, sugar bowl and teapot; this presentation immediately reminded me of when Olivia had produced the incredible tray in her sitting room at that fateful moment just before we discovered that Gerald was dead, unfortunately Olivia's presentation of the three levelled cake stand ladened with little finger cucumber sandwiches, a selection of biscuits, Dundee cake and four fruit scones with a pot of strawberry jam had been replaced, in this instance, by a small plate of assorted biscuits that the secretary placed on a side table and began pouring and serving our teas. I politely refused the biscuits. After she'd left, Mr. Jefferson continued as if we'd never been interrupted. He took from a file on his desk a sealed manilla envelope and handed it to me.

"Mrs. Armstrong specifically asked me to give this to you Mr. Collins." I took the envelope and held it in my fingers, uncertain as to whether it should be opened now or later. Mr. Jefferson sat quietly with his hands on the desk, he seemed to be waiting for me to open it, so I took a letter opener from the desk stand in front of me and gently sliced open the envelope and looked inside. I immediately recognised Olivia's joke, her final effort to make us squirm and then make us laugh, which is what we both did when I showed the contents to Joan, who also immediately recognised Olivia's copy of our 'Agreement'; the confession we'd feared may come back to haunt us at the hands of Mr. Jefferson.

"I have no idea as to the contents of the envelope, Mrs. Armstrong prepared and sealed it herself, but it obviously contains something that you appreciate and understand. The second duty I have is to advise you as to the instructions contained within her last Will and Testament, which I can summarise. He began to read.

"Mrs. Armstrong has appointed me as executor and has named you Mr. Brian Collins and you Mrs. Joan Collins as the sole beneficiaries. The extent of her estate in listed in Schedule Two." Mr. Jefferson turned a couple of pages before reading the contents. Joan took my hand and I don't think either of us heard the entire contents, I did hear some of details relating to her house, bank accounts and shares; it all sounded like such a huge amount of money and such a lot of assets. Neither of us could think of anything to say. When Mr. Jefferson finished reading the

Schedule he turned to the last page of the will and read a personal message that Olivia had written to them:-

"Thank you for changing my life in such a dramatic way, and for being my friend. I knew from the first time we met, on that memorable evening, that we were destined to share some important time together, I wish it could have been longer, but thank you for all the fun, excitement, love, care and memories you have given me, you completed my life. Now you must move forward with your lives and prepare a new and creative 'Retirement Plan'."

THE END.

I hope you've enjoyed THE RETIREMENT PLAN and would appreciate you giving it a star rating at the end of the following pages. Thanks.

WEBSITE: - www.jklambauthor.com

ALL OUR BOOKS – Please *click* title for more details.

SERIES---

The Coulson Boys – ADAM - Book 1.

The Coulson Boys – DANIEL - Book 2.

The Coulson Boys – HARRY - Book 3.

SEQUELS---

GEOFFREY – Book 1.

THE BOOK CLUB – Book 2.

⊷&⊶

HOW TO KILL YOUR WIFE – Book 1.

A SIMPLE MISTAKE – Book 2.

STAND ALONE---

THE GAME OF LIFE.

Printed in Great Britain
by Amazon